wondergirls™

Birthday Blues

D1096386

Jillian Brooks

SCHOLASTIC INC.
New York Toronto London Auckland Sydney
Mexico City New Delhi Hong Kong Buenos Aires

ISBN 0-439-45141-8

Copyright © 2003 17th Street Productions,
an Alloy, Inc. company
All rights reserved.
Published by Scholastic Inc.

 Produced by 17th Street Productions,
an Alloy, Inc. company
151 West 26th Street
New York, NY 10001

12 11 10 9 8 7 6 5 4 3 2 1   3 4 5 6 7 8/0

Printed in the U.S.A.   40
First Scholastic printing, February 2003

chapter
ONE

From My Book of Lists, by Felicia Fiol

<u>List #32: The Best Things About Turning 12</u>

1. I'm one year closer to being a teenager.
2. I get to have a party—a small one.
3. I have three best friends to invite to my party.
4. My mom makes the best birthday cake around.
5. My dad might get me a new watch like the silver one that Arielle wore to school the other day.
6. If he doesn't, maybe my mom will.
7. I'll get to stay up later. Maybe. On weekends.
8. I might start getting a bigger allowance. Although probably not.

"Did you see that little boy's face when Quentin jumped into his lap?" Traci asked as she spread out her sleeping bag. I smiled, and so did Amanda and Arielle. It was hard not to when we were talking about Quentin.

He's this little brown dog we've been taking to the Wonder Lake Hospital as part of our Healing Paws

1

program. We try to bring different animals from my dad's shelter each time, but Quentin almost always gets chosen. The kids really love him, and I guess we do, too.

"You know," Traci went on, "that boy was giggling so much when Quentin licked his face that I think he actually forgot he was in the hospital."

"That's what pet therapy is all about," Arielle said as she untied the thick black cords that held her sleeping bag together. Bringing animals into the hospital to cheer up patients had been her idea to begin with, but all four of us had worked together to make it happen.

"Yeah," Amanda agreed. "And that's why Quentin is a perfect therapy dog. He has great energy. He always makes people smile."

Great energy, I thought. It sounded like another phrase Amanda had borrowed from her baby-sitter, Penny. *Penny—who was dating my dad. Ugh*.

I mean, it's not like she's a bad person or anything. She's actually pretty nice—just a little . . . different. Flaky, really. But in an artistic sort of way. Still, I wasn't about to say anything bad about her. Not in front of Amanda, anyway. She loved Penny. Although Amanda wasn't exactly thrilled about the fact that Penny was dating my dad, either.

Amanda unrolled her bag and angled it so that her head would be near Traci's, and Arielle and I did the same. When we were finished, our sleeping bags were arranged like four petals on a huge flower with our pillows at the center. It was a perfect slumber party setup. We would be able to whisper and laugh as late as we wanted without waking up my mom, and that's important. She gets up at 3 A.M. to start the ovens in the bakery, so she's pretty big on getting her sleep. Which is why I was kind of surprised when she said I could have this slumber party.

Maybe it's because I'm almost twelve now, and she figures I'm a lot more mature. Or maybe it's because for the first time since she and dad got divorced two years ago, I actually have friends again. Close friends. *Best friends*. Either way, I was psyched when she said yes. But it also made me kind of nervous. My friends had spent lots of time at my dad's house but barely any at my mom's.

"Hey, Felicia—how old is Quentin, anyway?" Amanda asked.

"I'm not sure," I said. "I think he was something like four months old when my dad took him into the shelter, and he's been there for a while now."

"I'm surprised no one has adopted him yet," Traci said. "He's so cute."

"And friendly," Amanda added.

"And funny," I said.

"Don't forget *out of control*," Arielle put in. Traci and Amanda scowled at her. The way she had said it, it did sound kind of harsh, but I don't think she really meant it. I've seen her patting Quentin and talking baby talk to him enough times to know that she really likes him—even if she does make a big deal about his horrible dog breath whenever he licks her face.

"He's not out of control," Traci said. "He's just full of energy—he's still a puppy."

"Whatever," Arielle responded, flopping down on her sleeping bag.

Amanda flopped down next to her. "I know who should adopt Quentin," she said with a grin.

Arielle raised her eyebrows. "Who?"

"*You*," Amanda said. "You know you like him." Arielle squinted at her, but she didn't deny it.

"And he obviously likes you, too," Traci added as the two of us stretched out on our sleeping bags. We were all lying on our stomachs with our elbows propped on our pillows.

"That's for sure," I agreed. "He whimpers to get out of his cage and play with you every time you come over."

For a minute I thought I saw Arielle's green eyes light up, but then she rolled onto her back. "Yeah, well, I don't think he'd last very long at chez Davis," she said. "One set of muddy paw prints on my mom's Italian leather sofa and he'd be right back at your dad's shelter."

"That's too bad," Amanda and Traci said at almost

4

exactly the same time. And it was. But still, all I could think about was how cool it would be to have an Italian leather sofa. Arielle's house is full of cool furniture like that. She has this amazing white lace canopy bed with an embroidered bedspread that her parents got for her in France and an antique dresser with porcelain dolls arranged on top of it. I swear, her room could be photographed for an interior design magazine—her whole house could. My mom's apartment, on the other hand . . . well, let's just say no one from *Better Homes and Gardens* has been calling for an interview.

I glanced at my mother's ancient yellow-orange couch, wondering if Arielle and the others had noticed just how faded and worn it was. Or that the covers on the armrests were hiding actual holes in the upholstery. But even if they hadn't noticed how old the furniture was—my mom had bought most of it at yard sales when she and Dad split up—I'm sure they had all realized just how small the apartment was.

We'd barely been able to find enough space to fit all of our sleeping bags in one room. Finally, we had pushed all of the living room furniture back to the walls, but even then it was a tight fit. At Traci and Amanda's houses we'd been able to set everything up in their bedrooms. But my room at my mom's is barely big enough for its twin bed, desk, and bureau. Forget four sleeping bags—or even two. And my mom's bedroom isn't much bigger. Come to think of it, the whole place could probably fit into Arielle's gourmet kitchen—not that I care.

I mean, it's not really important to me how big my mom's apartment is or how cool her furniture looks or anything. And it's not that I think my friends care about that stuff, either. But still, this was the first time we'd had a slumber party at my mom's apartment, and I wanted everything to go well. I didn't want to be the one whose mother had the boring apartment with nothing to do and no room to goof around. I wanted my friends to have a good time. I wanted them to come back again.

"Hey—anyone up for a snack?" my mother called, interrupting my thoughts. We all whirled around just in time to see her coming through the door that led up from the bakery. She had a tray of chocolate éclairs in one hand and a bulging pastry bag in the other.

"Definitely!" Traci called. She scrambled to her feet and followed my mother into the dining room faster than Quentin could squirm out of his kennel. Amanda jumped up and hurried after her, and I started to go, too, but instead I stopped myself and waited for Arielle. She's always so cool about everything, so in control. It's easy to see why she's one of the most popular girls at Wonder Lake Middle School. Even in pajamas, she looked like she'd stepped right out of a teen magazine.

She was wearing light blue cotton boxers with little clouds all over them and a white cotton camisole. She even had matching pale blue slippers with a slight heel. I eyed my red plaid flannel pants and coordinating top and made a mental note to get some new pajamas as soon as possible. Maybe with some of my birthday money. If I got any.

Arielle and I walked out to the dining room, where my mother was setting everything out on the large rectangular cherry table that has long benches on each side for seating. She'd gotten that at a yard sale, too, but it was pretty nice. And with chairs at each end, she could fit a lot of people for dinner.

"Let's see. I have chocolate éclairs with cream filling, chocolate cream cheese brownies, and a few jelly doughnuts."

"Wow," Amanda said, staring at the spread. Her pink pajamas had a batik flower pattern, and the pants were cut like bell-bottomed capris. It wasn't a look that just anyone could pull off, but it fit Amanda perfectly. That was why she could say stuff like "Quentin has great energy" and sound totally believable.

"Did you say chocolate cream cheese?" Arielle asked, her eyes widening.

"Right here," my mom said, pointing at the brownies.

Arielle took one and placed it neatly on a napkin. "These look great, Mrs. Fiol," she said politely.

"They *are* great," Traci gushed, finishing up her first big bite.

"And the éclairs are, too," Amanda added. Then she turned to me. "You're so lucky that your mom runs a bakery, Felicia."

"Yeah," Traci agreed, stuffing another bite of brownie into her mouth. "And your dad runs an animal shelter. Your parents have the best houses for hanging out."

"That's for sure," Amanda agreed. Arielle didn't say anything. It looked like she was too focused on her brownie.

My mom smiled and thanked them for the compliments, but I just blinked a couple of times and stared. "Thanks," I said finally, wondering if they really meant it or if they were just saying that stuff because my mom was in the room. I mean, I guess it's true that my parents have pretty cool jobs, but did Amanda and Traci honestly prefer this tiny apartment and my dad's noisy shelter to the Davises' huge, perfectly designed house?

I glanced at my mom's faded jeans, her white T-shirt, and her dark green Fiol's Bakery apron, which was covered in flour. Her work clothes. They were nothing like the perfectly tailored skirts and jackets Mrs. Davis wore. But I guess Amanda had a point. There *were* benefits to having a mom who ran a bakery. *Benefits like jelly doughnuts*, I thought, grabbing an extra-sugary one.

"So how did your hospital visit go?" my mom asked once we were all sitting around the table.

"Awesome," Traci answered right away. "Everyone really seemed to enjoy the animals." The rest of us were still nibbling, but she'd already scarfed down her whole brownie. The way she ate, it amazed me that she was so thin. But then she was pretty active, too. Between sports, orchestra, and helping out at the shelter, she barely ever sat still. Forget Quentin. *Traci* had great energy.

"Yeah, I was talking to Mr. Chang, the hospital director," Arielle added, "and he said he really thinks our visits make a big difference with some of the patients."

"I'm sure they do," my mom replied. "Your visits are probably the most exciting part of the week for a lot of those patients. Staying in a hospital can be pretty dull—trust me, I know."

I scrunched my eyebrows together and dabbed the sugar off my lips with a napkin. "When were you ever in the hospital?" I asked.

My mother widened her eyes. "You mean I never told you that story?" I shook my head. "Oh. Well, it was when I was in high school," my mother began. "I was on the girls' softball team, and we were playing for the state championship."

Oh, no. She was going to tell one of her childhood stories. I didn't mind them when it was just the two of us, but did she really think my friends wanted to hear her life history? No one else's parents had hung out with us and told stories at our slumber parties. They'd all just left us alone. *Please let this be a short one*, I thought, chewing on my pinky nail. But something about the way my mom was leaning forward with an excited gleam in her eye told me it wasn't going to be.

"The game was tied one-one in the bottom of the ninth," she went on, "and I had managed to get on base with a single. After that, the next two batters on my team struck out, so we had two outs against us. But fortunately, I was able to steal second *and* third during their ups. So then it all came down to Martha Hamlin—she was our cleanup hitter and could usually be counted on for at least a double, but this pitcher was really tough. Still, if Martha could just get a single, I knew that I might be able to get home, and then we'd win without having to go into extra innings."

I stared at my mother, my mouth slightly open. Why hadn't she ever told me this story before? It was definitely one of her better ones. Still, I couldn't help feeling like my friends must think she was really weird, just sitting down and talking to us like this was *her* slumber party, too. I hoped she was almost done.

"So what happened?" Traci asked. "Did Martha get you home?"

My mother tilted her head to the side. "Sort of," she said. "Martha had a full count—three balls and two strikes—so it all came down to that last pitch, and it was a good one. Even from third base I could tell it was a perfect fastball—low, but definitely in the strike zone. And Martha knew it, too. She took a swing . . . and missed, but the catcher dropped the ball."

"That means the batter can run," Traci blurted.

"Exactly," my mother said with a grin.

"What do you mean?" Amanda asked.

"Well, if the catcher drops the ball on the third strike, the batter can try to run to first," my mother explained. "And of course any other players on base can run, too."

"So did you do it? Did you steal home?" Arielle asked. I glanced over at her, surprised to see her keen green eyes trained on my mother. I couldn't believe it. She really seemed interested.

"I ran," my mom said, smiling. "And it was close, but I slid into home, and I was safe."

"That's so cool," Traci said.

Arielle nodded. "You won the state championship for your team."

"Well, I don't know about that," my mom said. "But I did manage to break my leg when I slid. *In two places*. I was in traction in the hospital for three weeks before they let me go back to school in a cast. But I did get all the cute boys to sign it," she added with a smirk.

"*Mom,*" I said.

"Oh, Felicia—don't tell me you haven't discovered boys yet. I've seen the posters in your room."

"*Mom!*" I yelled, cringing as Arielle, Amanda, and Traci giggled. I glared at my mother, and she got the hint.

"All right, it looks like I've overstayed my welcome," she said. "I just have a few things to finish up in the bakery, and then I'll go to my room and stay out of your hair." I scowled at her as she left, but she didn't seem to notice.

"So, Felicia," Arielle said once my mom had disappeared down the stairs. "Is it true that you've discovered boys?" Amanda and Traci burst out laughing.

"I can't believe she said that," I muttered. "My mom is so lame."

"No, she's not," Traci said once she had stopped giggling. "Your mom's cool."

"Totally," Amanda agreed. "Those were the best slumber party snacks I've ever had."

"And her softball story was great. She was really athletic, wasn't she?" Traci asked.

"I guess," I responded. I knew she'd played field hockey, basketball, and softball in high school, but I guess I'd just never really thought much about it before. Somehow I had a hard time picturing her as . . . *young.*

"That's awesome," Arielle said. "My mother didn't

do any sports. She was too busy running for president of every club she could join."

"That's cool. I bet your mom was really popular," I said. *Just like you.*

"Maybe," Arielle said with a shrug. "But she never slid into home to win a state championship."

Wow. I couldn't believe it. All of my friends—even Arielle—seemed to think my mom was okay. I stopped chewing on my nails and tried to relax a little. It was, after all, a slumber party. It was supposed to be fun—not stressful.

"So, Felicia," Arielle began with a slight smirk. "Does your mother know you have a *boyfriend?*"

"Who? Patrick?" I asked.

"No—Mr. Metcalf, the boys' basketball coach," Arielle sneered. "Of course I mean Patrick."

My eyes got really wide, and I didn't know what to say. I mean, yeah, I thought Patrick was cute and all, and we had been hanging out together a lot, but still.

"Well, she *knows* him," I said finally. "But, um, I'm not sure I'd call him my . . . *boyfriend.*"

Arielle sniffed. "Why not?" she asked. "He's a boy and he's your friend, isn't he?"

"Well, yeah, but—" I blinked and looked away.

"Cut it out, Arielle," Amanda said. "Can't you tell you're making Felicia uncomfortable?"

"I am not," Arielle replied, tossing her auburn hair over her shoulder.

"Yes, you are," Amanda insisted. "And besides, just because she spends time with Patrick doesn't mean he's her boyfriend. Ryan Bradley is a boy and he's your friend, but he's not your boyfriend, is he?"

"No," Arielle said. "He's Traci's."

Now it was Traci's turn to look shocked. "I don't think so," she said.

"Oh, yes, he is," Arielle said, rolling her eyes. "Just like your brother, Dave, is Amanda's."

"Arielle! What's wrong with you?" Amanda demanded, but Arielle just laughed.

"What's wrong with all of *you* is more like it," she said. "You've all got crushes on guys who are obviously crushing on you, too, but none of you will admit it. Can you say *lame?*"

I felt my cheeks getting hot and hoped my embarrassment didn't show. But just having Arielle refer to Patrick as my boyfriend had made me feel totally self-conscious. *Was* he my boyfriend? And if he was, what did that mean? Was I supposed to walk to classes with him or hold his hand or . . . *kiss* him? The idea gave me goose bumps. I wasn't sure I was ready for any of that. I stared down at the remaining snacks on the table, trying to avoid Arielle's gaze. Amanda and Traci, on the other hand, were glaring at her.

"I think someone's jealous," Amanda said, folding her arms across her chest.

"I think you're right," Traci agreed, doing the same.

"Excuse me?" Arielle said.

"You're just upset because you don't have a guy to hang around with and we all do," Amanda said, staring straight into Arielle's green eyes.

Gulp. My heart jumped into my throat. Worrying what my friends would think of my mom's apartment had been bad enough. The last thing I needed was for them to start fighting again—at my slumber party, no less.

"Um, does anyone want something to drink? Some milk or soda?" I asked, but it was like they hadn't even heard me.

"You've got to be kidding," Arielle said without blinking. "You think I'm jealous of *Ryan*, *Patrick*, and *Dave*?" The way she'd said their names, even I started to feel a little offended, but I still didn't want a fight.

"Boy, that doughnut made me thirsty," I said, clearing my throat exaggeratedly.

"Yeah, I do think you're jealous," Amanda said, completely ignoring me. Obviously I wasn't going to be able to distract them. So instead I gnawed at my thumbnail and waited. *Please don't get angry at each other. Not here. Not now*, I prayed.

"Well, I'm not," Arielle said. Traci looked like she was about to object, but Arielle cut her off. "Don't get me wrong," she said. "Ryan, Patrick, and Dave are all . . . cute. They're just not exactly *my* type."

"And who is your type?" Traci asked.

"I'm not sure," Arielle said. "I guess I haven't

found him yet. But that's okay. I wouldn't want to be tied down to one guy. It's more fun to play the field. That way I can flirt with whoever I want without worrying about anyone getting upset."

Phew, I thought, relieved to see Amanda and Traci sitting back in their seats. For a second there I had thought they were going to pounce on Arielle, but instead it looked like they were going to just let her comments slide.

"Besides," Arielle added with a sigh, "I could have any guy I wanted at any time. So I really don't have any reason to be jealous."

I watched as Amanda and Traci both sat bolt upright. Now, that was a comment they weren't going to ignore. I had to do something—quick. But what?

"Hey," I called just as I saw Amanda's lips parting to speak. "Next Friday is my birthday, and I'm having a party."

All three of my friends turned and stared at me like I was crazy, and I really couldn't blame them. I'd blurted out the sentence in one quick breath.

"Next Friday is your birthday?" Amanda said. "I didn't even know it was coming up."

"I did," Traci said. "I mean, I knew it was this month, at least, but I thought it was still a couple of weeks away. Why didn't you say something before?"

"I don't know." I shrugged. "I guess I forgot."

Arielle raised her eyebrows. "You forgot your own birthday?"

"Sort of," I replied, and in a way I had. Not the fact that it was coming up, but that my mom had said I could have a party. I'd been meaning to mention it, but I just kept forgetting to bring it up. I guess after so many years of not having friends to invite over for stuff like that, I'd kind of gotten out of practice. "So . . . do you guys want to come?"

"Yeah," Amanda said.

"Definitely," Traci added. Arielle just nodded.

"When did you say? Friday night?" Traci asked.

"Yeah. It's kind of a dinner thing," I said. "My mom's going to order a bunch of pizzas and bake a cake and stuff, so, like, five o'clock?"

"Sounds good," Amanda said. "And I bet your mom makes the best birthday cake in town."

"Yeah, I can hardly wait," Traci said. "Is there anything we can do to help out?"

"I have a bunch of party invitations left over from my birthday bash last year," Arielle said. "I could bring them to school tomorrow so you could hand them out."

"Actually," I said, glancing around the tiny apartment, "we're having it here, so it's going to be a pretty small party."

"That's okay," Arielle said with a shrug. "We'll just invite the cute guys."

"Well, the thing is," I started, not quite sure how to say it. Arielle was used to throwing huge parties and inviting everyone in the school. She was bound to find my little get-together boring. "I'm not sure if . . ." I jammed my already worn down thumbnail back between my teeth.

"What is it, Felicia?" Amanda asked.

"It's just that—" Boy, did I feel stupid. "I think it's just going to be the four of us. And my mom."

"Oh," Arielle said. *I knew it. She thinks I'm totally lame*, I thought. There was no way she was going to want to come. "Well, that's cool. Still—let me know if you need any help with decorations or anything. My mom has a friend who does the best ice sculptures. I think I'm going to have him do a few for my birthday party, as centerpieces at the food tables."

Amanda frowned at her. "Arielle—your birthday isn't until April."

"I know, but it's never too early to start planning," Arielle told her. "Especially since *my* birthday party is going to be the biggest and best one ever to hit Wonder Lake." Amanda and Traci both scowled at her, and I think Amanda may even have kicked her under the table. "Ow!" she muttered, then she turned toward me. "Anyway, I'm sure yours is going to be fun, too, Felicia," she added.

I think Traci and Amanda kind of expected me to be upset, but I just smiled. I didn't mind if Arielle's party *was* the biggest and best birthday party Wonder Lake ever saw. I was just happy that my three best friends were coming to mine.

chapter
TWO

<u>Welcome to Fiol's Bakery</u>
Today's Freshly Baked Breads:
  Whole Wheat, White, Pumpernickel, Rye, Sesame, Wheat, & Marble

Today's Muffins:
  Blueberry, Cranberry, Bran, Lemon Poppy Seed, Pumpkin Spice, Chocolate Chip, & Cinnamon

Today's Brews:
  Breakfast Blend (reg & decaf), Hazelnut Cream, Mocha Java, Colombian, French Roast

"These lemon poppy seed muffins are the best," Amanda said. "Does your mom ever give out her recipes?"

"I don't think so," I said, glancing toward the back of the bakery. Things were pretty quiet right now—just the four of us at one table and a young couple reading the Sunday paper over coffee and bagels at another. But in about a half hour it would be a zoo.

That's why my mom was out in the kitchen. She was getting ready for the 11 A.M. rush. "Why?"

"I was just thinking that maybe she could pass along some tips to Penny," Amanda said. "You know—give her something to bake other than those corn-pumpkin muffins?" The two of us burst out laughing while Traci and Arielle just shook their heads.

The one time Amanda and I had been over to Penny's for dinner at the same time, she had served these corn-pumpkin muffins that we had both hated—Amanda, because she hated all things pumpkin, and me, because I was mad that my father had dragged me over there to get to know his new girlfriend. Of course, she wasn't his *new* girlfriend anymore. They'd been dating for more than two months, so now she was just his girlfriend. Unfortunately.

"Oh, hey—my mom's here," Traci said, nodding toward the street in front of the bakery. I looked through the picture window and saw Ms. McClintic's minivan parked next to the curb. Ms. McClintic leaned forward and waved, and Traci waved back. "I'm going to run out there before she comes in and starts talking your mom's ear off," she said, wrapping what was left of her raspberry Danish in a napkin and tightening the top on her orange juice. "If that happens, your mom will never be ready for the rush. Thanks a lot, Felicia," she said, standing to go. "I'll see you in school tomorrow."

"And there's your dad, Arielle," Amanda said, pointing at a black BMW that had just pulled up. "So we have to go, too. He is giving me a ride home, isn't he?"

Arielle glanced out and waved. "Yeah, but we don't have to worry about him coming in," she said. "He always waits in the car. Still, we should get out there pretty fast—before he starts beeping." She said it with a smile, but I knew she was serious. He beeped whenever he picked her up at the shelter.

"Okay. I'll see you all tomorrow," I said. "Amanda's locker before homeroom, right?" We met there just about every morning to check in and say hi before the school day started.

"Right," Amanda said, and Traci and Arielle nodded. Then they all headed for the door. I heard them call, "Thank you, Mrs. Fiol," as they passed the back counter, and my mom stuck her head out to wave good-bye.

After they were gone and the little bell above the door had stopped jingling, the bakery seemed way too quiet. It was like being in the mall at closing time, when they suddenly turned off all the music and every other row of lights so you'd know it was time to leave. And I was feeling really let down. Probably because I knew the only things I had to look forward to for the rest of the day were helping out in the bakery and finishing my homework.

Oh, well, I thought, picking up the leftover napkins from our table. *At least I already got my math problems out of the way*. I'd finished those in class on Friday when Mr. Reid had given us some quiet time to work. And that meant all I had to do for homework was an exercise in my Spanish book. Oh, and read a story and answer some questions about it for English. But still, not too bad.

I stuck the clean napkins from our table back in a stack next to the register and threw the dirty ones into the paper-only recycling bin. Then I walked behind the counter, tied on my green Fiol's Bakery apron, and headed for the kitchen.

"Felicia Fiol, reporting for duty," I said to my mom with a salute. "What can I do?" At the moment my mom was elbow deep in bread dough in the huge forty-quart bowl attached to her industrial-size mixer.

"There are two trays of muffins in the oven that are ready to come out," she said without even looking up. "And the pastries on the cooling racks are ready to bring out front."

"Okay," I said, getting right to work.

I had to hand it to my mom. She and my dad had started this bakery together five years ago, and she'd really made it work. Dad used to help out, too, and he was still part owner—even after the divorce—but my mom was the one who'd always been more involved. And for the last two years she'd been doing it on her own. She did all the baking and ran the café, too.

An older woman who I really liked, Blanche, came

in a few days a week to help out in front. She ran the register, kept the tables neat, stocked the shelves in the display cases, and took care of everything so that my mom could have a break. But aside from her, I was my mom's only helper.

I finished unloading the last of the cinnamon rolls into their rack and checked on all the coffee carafes to see which ones needed refilling. Then, after starting up a few of the coffeemakers, I headed back to the kitchen to see what else I could do.

My mom was shaping one last loaf of bread from the dough she'd just made and putting it in a pan. "There," she said, wiping her hands on her apron. "Did you get all of those pastries out?"

"Yup."

"Great. Well, if you could just check the coffee carafes—"

"Already done," I said, smiling proudly.

My mom cocked her head. "Coffee brewing?" she asked.

"Uh-huh."

My mother put her flour-covered hands on her hips and grinned at me. "My, my, my, Ms. Fiol. You'll be running this place by the time you're fifteen."

I hope not, I thought, but I just smiled. I didn't want my mom to get the wrong idea. Running a bakery was really cool and everything, but it wasn't exactly my dream. I wanted to be a lawyer—and not just because both of Arielle's parents were. Really. I'd been thinking about it for a while. Well, at least since the beginning of this school year.

"So, then," my mom said, sliding two trays of bread into the oven. "It looks like we're all set until the customers start pouring in." She untied her apron and threw it into the silver laundry bin, then tied on a fresh one. Together we walked out to the front counter, where my mom sat down at one of the bar stools.

I topped off my mother's coffee mug with decaf—she always preferred to go caffeine-free once she was done with the baking—and grabbed myself a carton of milk from the cooler. Then I took a seat next to her.

"Thanks," my mom said. She sipped some coffee, closed her eyes, and took a deep breath. The five minutes she had off between the early morning and late morning rush hours was her only chance to unwind. "So . . . how was your slumber party?" she asked.

"Fun," I said. "Thanks for letting me have it."

"You're welcome. I'm just glad I finally got a chance to say more than hello and good-bye to your new friends," she said. "Arielle and Amanda seem like really nice girls."

"They are," I told her. *And really popular, too*, I thought, but I wasn't going to say it to my mom. If I did, she'd tell me that kind of stuff doesn't matter. Adults always say things like that.

"And it must be nice to have Traci around," my

mother went on. "You girls used to have so much fun together during our summers on the Carolina coast."

"Yeah," I said, smiling. I'd known Traci for six years now, although for the last two we'd just been calling, writing, and e-mailing. I hadn't actually seen her since my parents and I stopped spending our summers in South Carolina after the divorce. But we'd spent four superfun summers together and kept in touch pretty well. Then this year her family moved out here to Wonder Lake, Illinois, so her father could help set up the new medical clinic. He's a pediatrician.

"It is cool having her here full-time," I said. "But I still really miss summers at the beach."

"There's a beach here," my mom said. She was talking about the recreation area the town had created a few years back. They'd taken a huge piece of land, dug it out, filled it with water, trucked in some sand, and made their own beach. It was nice, but it wasn't an ocean.

"I know, but it's not the same," I replied.

"No, I suppose not," my mom admitted, taking another sip of coffee. She sighed, and I couldn't help thinking she looked a little sad. Then her face brightened. "Do you remember that time we all went out to dinner at that little seafood shack just down the road from our cottage?" she asked.

I smiled right away—I knew exactly the night she was thinking of. "Mm-hmm." I nodded. "When Dad and Mr. McClintic had a contest to see who could eat the most raw oysters?"

My mother brought her mug to her lips, then set it down. "Yes—and neither one of them wanted to be the first to give up," she said, beginning to laugh, "so the waiter had to bring tray after tray of oysters to our table until finally the entire waitstaff was gathered around, watching them."

"And everyone else in the restaurant started watching, too," I added, remembering how embarrassed Traci and I had been until we realized that the crowd was actually cheering them on. "Who finally won, anyway?" I asked. Somehow I couldn't recall that particular detail.

"I think it was a tie," my mother said, chuckling. "Mostly because after thirty-something oysters each, they both felt too sick to continue. Although I think it was actually the Tabasco sauce that did your father in—I can still see the sweat running down the sides of his forehead."

I laughed. It had been a really fun night, and I remembered Traci and I talking afterward about how cool both of our dads were. And how gross raw oysters were. I glanced over at my mother, who had begun sipping at her coffee again.

"Those were fun times," she said quietly, staring at the chalkboard, where the daily breads, muffins, and coffees were always listed. Actually, though, she seemed to be staring past it. And I couldn't help thinking that she looked a little sad again. Although not sad, exactly.

What was that vocabulary word we had last week in English class? Something with a *w*. I know—*wistful*, that was it. And that was how my mom looked. *Wistful*. Like she really missed those summers on the coast and wished she could have them back again. But that wasn't possible, was it?

She and my dad had been apart for two years now, and neither one of them had ever said anything about the possibility of getting back together again. But I swear, the way my mom looked right at that moment, it almost seemed like she missed him. Or at least like she missed our family vacations. But even if she did, it wasn't like it would make any difference. My dad had moved on—with Penny, of all people.

It was kind of funny, though. For the past two years I'd always thought that if I could snap my fingers and put everything back to the way it used to be, I'd do it in a second. Now I realized that I'd just settle for my dad dumping Penny. Like I said, it's not that she's a bad person or anything. It's just that the last thing I needed was a crystal-wearing, corn-pumpkin-muffin-baking, papier-mâché-animal artist for a stepmother.

chapter
THREE

Excerpt from Traci's diary

Ideas for Felicia's Birthday Present
1. Obviously not a pet.
   She has enough animals running around at her dad's shelter to last a lifetime.
2. New Shauna Ferris CD?
   No. Arielle's been playing hers so much, Felicia's probably already sick of it. I know I am.
3. Nail polish?
   With the way she bites her nails? No way.
4. Earrings?
   Kind of lame.
5. Friendship bracelet? Double lame.
   I've known Felicia for years, but this is the first time I'm going to be around for her birthday. I need to do something really special for her. But what?

I tried to walk calmly to Amanda's locker—cool and in control, the way Arielle would have been—but I was way too excited. Especially when I saw that the others were already there.

"Guess what!" I blurted, jogging the last few steps.

"What?"

"I talked to my mom last night, and she said I could invite four boys to my party, too! Isn't that great? It's going to be kind of cramped, I know, but having boys kind of makes it feel like more of a party. Not that it wouldn't be a party with you guys or anything," I added quickly. "I just mean—" *What did I mean?* I was babbling so fast, I barely even knew what I was saying.

"We know what you mean," Traci said, saving me from myself. "Having more people does make a party more exciting."

"Right," Amanda agreed. Then she glanced around the group and giggled. "Especially when they're boys," she added. Of course, Traci and I started giggling, too, but Arielle rolled her eyes. I'm sure she thought we were being really immature, but for once I didn't care. I was too excited. Suddenly, my birthday party was beginning to feel like an event. And the fact that I hadn't done anything really special for it in the last few years made it seem even more exciting.

"So who are you inviting?" Arielle asked. "Which boys?"

"Well," I said, suddenly feeling self-conscious about the idea. It was one thing to say I was going to have four boys there. It was another thing to single out the ones I wanted to invite. "I guess I'll probably invite Patrick," I said.

"Obviously." Arielle groaned. But thankfully, she didn't say anything about him being my boyfriend. I would have been mortified if anyone had overheard her saying something like that. "Who else?"

"Well," I said again, clearing my throat. "I sort of thought I'd let you guys decide the other three."

"Cool," Arielle said, nodding. I was dying to know who she would invite, but she was squinting up at the ceiling, tapping her index finger against her lips, like she was concentrating on something, and I didn't dare ask. Instead I looked at Traci.

"Um," she said, glancing first at Amanda and then at me. "I guess . . . Ryan."

"Okay," I said. I was kind of glad Arielle wasn't paying attention. That meant she wouldn't be teasing Traci about her choice.

"How about you, Amanda?" I asked.

Amanda grinned a little, then looked over at Traci. "Would it be weird for you to have your brother there, too?" she asked.

Traci shrugged. "Nah. Anyway, he'll be on his best behavior with you around."

Amanda smiled. "Okay, then. I'll invite Dave." The three of us grinned and giggled at the idea of having all of our crushes in one place together. It was sort of like a triple date, except for the fact that none of us were allowed to actually date yet. Then almost all at the same time we turned to Arielle, who was still staring at the ceiling.

I'm not even sure she had been listening while Traci and Amanda had made their choices, but like I said, that was just as well. If she had, she definitely would have taken the chance to tease them. Or maybe congratulate them for finally doing something about their crushes. As it was, she'd said nothing. But now as she stood there, just staring off into space, I was starting to feel really uneasy. And I could tell Amanda and Traci were uncomfortable, too.

The three of us looked back and forth between Arielle and each other. Why was she just standing there? Why wasn't she saying anything? Had all of this talk about boys actually started to upset her? What an idiot I was. I'd been so excited about being able to invite boys to my party that I'd forgotten all about the fact that Arielle didn't have anyone to invite.

Amanda widened her eyes at both me and Traci, pressing her lips together. I knew what she was thinking. I was thinking the same thing. Was Arielle starting to feel left out because she was the only one without a . . . well, in *her* words, a boyfriend? Traci bit her lip. Someone had to say something and soon.

"Arielle?" Amanda said quietly. "Are you all right?"

Arielle shook her head like Amanda had awakened her from a daydream. "Huh? Oh, yeah. Why?" Amanda stole a glance at me and Traci.

"Because you just zoned out for like five minutes," Traci said. It wasn't exactly tactful, but it was true.

Arielle studied each of our faces for a second, looking serious, but then she laughed. "I guess I did," she said. "But you would, too, if you were trying to pick just *one* cute guy to invite to Felicia's party." Traci arched an eyebrow. "I mean, it's easy for *you*," Arielle continued, meeting Traci's skeptical gaze. "And Amanda and Felicia, too. You all know who you have to invite. But I have so many guys to choose from."

"Who we *have* to invite?" Traci said, scowling.

"You know what I mean," Arielle replied. "It's like I said Saturday night—the three of you are already tied down, but I'm free to play the field."

"Not this again." Traci moaned, but Arielle ignored her.

"There are so many possibilities that I just can't decide," Arielle went on. "Except that I'm pretty sure it will be an eighth grader. I've had my eye on a couple of them for a while now, and a party is always a great opportunity to get together with someone new."

Amanda and Traci both seemed a little put off by Arielle's attitude, but I was relieved. For a moment there I had actually thought that she was upset, but now I could see that she was fine.

"Maybe Scott Duncan or Mike Repp," Arielle murmured, thinking aloud. "Or Brian McFee. He's been majorly flirty with me on the bus lately."

"Come on—we better get to homeroom," Traci said.

She, Amanda, and Arielle turned to go. "See you

later, Felicia," they all called. Unfortunately, my homeroom was in the opposite direction. But that was okay. I had plenty to think about on my way there. Like having Brian McFee—one of the most popular guys in the eighth grade—at my birthday party. Singing "Happy Birthday" to *me*—shy, boring Felicia Fiol. How incredible would that be?

I knew Traci and Amanda thought Arielle had gone a bit overboard the other night when she'd said she could have any guy she wanted at any time. But I, for one, believed her. And I couldn't wait to see who she was going to bring to my party.

chapter
FOUR

Excerpt from Felicia's diary

Dear Diary—
Arielle told me in Spanish class that she's pretty sure she's going to bring Brian McFee on Friday. I hope he has a good time. I'd hate for him to be bored and think I'm a total loser. But then he won't really be paying attention to me, anyway. Not with Arielle there.

She's so cool. So confident. If I had been in her position this morning—the only girl without an obvious guy to invite—I would have totally freaked. I would have felt so left out that I probably would have made some excuse to avoid the party altogether. But not Arielle. She can handle anything.

"Yuck," Arielle said, staring into the pen where Quentin and a few other dogs were kept together. "Rabbit pellets, I can handle. But someone else is going to have to clean *that* up."

I put down the water bottle I'd been trying to attach to the ferrets' cage and walked over to where she was standing. "That *is* pretty bad," I agreed, although I'd seen a lot worse. But there was no reason to point that out to Arielle. She'd come a long way already just being able to talk about rabbit poop. A few short weeks ago even that would have grossed her out.

"Don't worry—I'll take care of it," Traci said. She opened the door and headed right in, pooper-scooper in one hand, plastic bag in the other. Unlike Arielle, she was an animal lover all the way, and nothing about them grossed her out at all. Arielle and I watched as she moved around the pen methodically, taking care of one area after another until it was tidied up.

"There," she said, coming back out. "You *can* handle putting in fresh straw for their beds, can't you?" she asked Arielle.

"Very funny, McClintic," Arielle said. Then she pointed at the plastic bag, which was now full. "You know, I think you've found your calling." I giggled, but Traci just shook her head and headed for the compost heap out back.

"You want to help me with the straw?" Arielle asked.

"Sure," I said. "Just let me finish with this water bottle." I headed back to the ferrets' cage, which was just inside my dad's big barn. It only took me a minute to get the bottle fastened on, and then Arielle and I headed toward the back to grab a few armfuls of straw. We were just making our way back to the dog pens when a figure walking up the path from the house caught my eye. "Ugh," I moaned.

"Huh?" Arielle asked, but then she turned and saw what I was looking at. "Oh. How nice," she muttered sarcastically.

"Hi, girls," Penny cooed, wrinkling her nose as she grinned at us. I swear, she acted like we were kindergartners or something.

"Hi, Penny," I said. Arielle just nodded and raised her eyebrows a little. It was a greeting without words. A cold shoulder without the cold. Or the shoulder.

"Where's Amanda?"

"Oh, she's over at the pond feeding the ducks," I said, "but—"

"Penny!" Amanda called, jogging up the path, followed closely by Traci, who'd obviously gone over to help her after dumping the poop.

"Hi, Penny," Traci said, almost as enthusiastically. The two of them seemed to think Penny was the coolest person in the world. Thankfully, Arielle was in agreement with me. Penny wasn't cool. She was weird.

"Amanda, Traci," Penny gushed, spreading her arms wide for a hug. "It's so good to see both of you." She gave both of them that same wrinkly-nose smile she'd given me and Arielle. I guessed it was just her regular way of smiling, but that didn't make me like it any better.

"You too," Amanda said after she'd given Penny her hug. "What are you doing here? Are you and Mr. Fiol going out tonight?"

"We are *later*," Penny said, which I already knew. My dad had asked me if I wanted to go with them, but I had assured him I'd be fine staying home alone. "But right now I'm here to pick you up, silly. Are you almost ready to go?"

Silly. If I were Amanda, I would have cringed, but she didn't seem to mind.

"Oh, shoot," Amanda said, glancing at Traci. "I'm sorry, Penny. I told my mom I'd call you, but I guess I forgot."

"Why? What's wrong?" Penny asked, squinting.

"Nothing's *wrong*," Amanda said. "It's just that you don't have to pick me up tonight."

"I don't?" Penny said.

"No," Amanda said, looking apologetically at Penny. "Ms. McClintic is picking me up tonight because I'm having dinner at Traci's house. I'm really sorry I forgot to call."

"Oh, that's okay," Penny said, waving one hand. That's how weird she is. Any normal person would have been annoyed about having driven all the way across town when they didn't actually need to, but Penny didn't seem to mind at all. "I had a nice drive out here. The sunlight is always so pretty at this time of day."

Arielle turned to me and mouthed the words *space case*. I started to giggle but managed to stop myself after just a little bit of a snorting noise. Amanda and

Traci both turned toward me suspiciously, but I forced myself to keep a straight face, and eventually they looked away again.

"So you're having dinner with Traci and her cute brother, Dane, hmmm?" Penny asked. Amanda blushed at the mention of Traci's brother, even though Penny had gotten his name wrong.

"That's *Dave*," Arielle said, earning a scowl from Traci and Amanda.

"Oh, right—Dave," Penny repeated, wrinkling her nose at Arielle. "Thanks, sweetie."

"Anytime," Arielle said, and I'm sure she meant it. She loved correcting Penny.

"Well, that will be fun for you," Penny said. "But, hey, since I'm here . . . is there anything I can help with?"

I glanced toward the dog pens, a little disappointed that there weren't any really big dogs at the shelter right now. Penny used to be scared of all dogs, no matter what size they were, and for a while I had hoped that my dad would have to dump her because of it. After all, the animals at his shelter were his life, and fifty percent of them were dogs.

But we'd been getting Penny used to them slowly, starting with the small ones and working our way up. She was actually pretty good around the really small ones now—like the Chihuahua, Max. And she'd even gotten used to Quentin, who was getting bigger every day. But larger dogs, like full-grown goldens, Labs, and shepherds, still scared her. Too bad we didn't have any.

"I don't think so," I said. "We're just about done, really. Arielle and I just have to fix up the dog beds, and then that's it."

"You can help us feed the ducks," Amanda said. Her brown paper bag of feed was still half full.

"Oh. Okay," Penny said, but just as she, Traci, and Amanda were about to skip down the path to the pond, my father came out.

"Penny," he said. "I thought I heard your voice. What are you doing here? It's not six o'clock already, is it?"

"Oh, no—not even close, Luis," Penny said. "I'm afraid I just got my schedule a little mixed up."

"What—*you?*" my father teased, and Penny started to giggle. I thought I was going to throw up.

"Actually, it was my fault, Mr. Fiol," Amanda said. "I forgot to call Penny to let her know she didn't have to pick me up today."

"But I don't mind," Penny put in quickly. "In fact, I've just had a great idea," she said, putting her hand on my dad's forearm. I hated it when she did that. "Why don't I hang out with the girls until it's time for them to go, and then we can head out early for dinner—like around five o'clock? Is that about when your mom will be here, Traci?"

39

"Yup," Traci said.

Penny turned back to my dad. "What do you say, Luis?"

My dad smiled at Penny but shook his head. "I'm afraid I can't," he said. "I need to stay until six just in case someone stops by to drop off a new animal or adopt one."

"Oh, of course," Penny said. "Sometimes I forget that you're on your own here—except for your volunteers, of course," she added, smiling at me and my friends. Traci and Amanda smiled back. Arielle and I both sighed.

"Maybe you should consider hiring some part-time help so that you're not the only person who can open and close the shelter," Penny went on.

I almost snorted. My dad, hire help? Yeah, right. Even if he did, he'd still find some reason to spend all of his time looking out for the animals. Like I said before—the shelter is his life.

"That would be nice," my dad said, causing my jaw to drop open. I'd never even heard him consider the idea before. "Unfortunately," he went on, "I think I've already gotten all the grant money I'm going to get for this year. For now I'll just have to rely on my faithful volunteers."

"We won't let you down, Mr. Fiol," Traci said, beaming up at him. "It's just too bad we're not old enough to run things without you around. Then we could give you a break."

"Trust me, Traci—the four of you do plenty around here. And you *do* give me a break."

"Yeah, but you can't actually *leave* when we're the only ones here," Amanda said. "At least not for very long. Maybe we should start advertising for some adult volunteers—"

My dad's laughter interrupted her midsentence. "I tell you, Penny," he said, "these girls are amazing. If it weren't for child labor laws, they'd be running the place."

Penny smiled and nodded, looking directly at Amanda. "Yes, they are amazing," she agreed. "And they're also smart. Why *don't* you advertise for an adult volunteer or two? Then you'd be able to get away early once in a while or leave during the day to take care of other things."

"That would be great," my father said. "The problem is that I've already put an ad in the paper for volunteers. In fact, I've run three separate ads over the last two months. And the chamber of commerce has my information, too, just in case anyone inquires about volunteering in the community. Unfortunately, there haven't been any responses."

"Hmph," Penny grunted. "Well, maybe you need to make it a *paid* part-time position instead of a volunteer one."

"I'd love to," my father said, surprising me again. It was the first I'd heard about him wanting or needing more help. "But as I said, the shelter just doesn't have the money for that."

"If money's the issue," Penny said, "I could help you out. I've got a little extra cash—"

My father put up his hand. "Penny, I couldn't ask you to do that," he said.

"You don't have to ask," Penny told him with a smile. "I'm offering. Now, how much would it take to—"

"Uh, Penny," my father said. "I really don't think it would be a good idea to have you paying the salary of one of my employees."

"Oh, but I wouldn't be—*you* would. I'd just make a large donation to the shelter, and then you could use it however you wanted to."

I'm not sure if my mouth dropped open again or if I had just never closed it, but either way, I knew I was gaping. Had I heard her right? Penny wanted to make a big donation to the shelter? Since when was she rolling in dough? Apparently, Arielle was wondering the same thing because she, too, was staring at Penny.

My father tilted his head to one side and scratched his neck. "Penny, I don't think—"

"Oh, come on, Luis—people make donations to non-profit organizations all the time. It's not like I'd be—"

"*Penny,*" my father cut in, his tone growing a little deeper. He glanced at me and my friends, then cleared his throat. "Why don't we go into my office to discuss this? I think the girls have a few things to finish up before Ms. McClintic gets here."

"Oh. All right," Penny said, sounding puzzled. "But . . . I don't understand. What do we have to discuss? I can just write a check right now, and then—" She stiffened as my father placed his hand on her elbow and nudged her toward the house. "Oh. Um . . . okay," Penny said, shuffling along with him. "I guess we'll talk about it inside." He had obviously caught her by surprise—along with the rest of us.

"Whoa," Arielle said when they were out of sight. "That was serious."

"What was serious—their conversation?" Traci asked.

"No, Penny's hairdo," Arielle sneered. "Yes—of course their conversation."

"Why?" Traci asked.

"Because it was just about to turn into an argument," Arielle explained.

"Do you think so?" I asked.

"Definitely," Arielle said, nodding. "Listen." She gestured toward the house, where my dad's office was, and we all went silent. Sure enough, we could just hear my dad and Penny talking, and it seemed obvious that they were talking kind of loud. The way people did when they were arguing.

I cupped my hands behind my ears, trying to make out what they were saying, but it was no use. I was just about to give up when Arielle crouched down and went sneaking up to the house.

"Arielle!" Traci whisper-yelled, but Arielle just waved

her off and continued toward my father's office window.

"I can't believe her," Traci muttered. "She shouldn't be listening in on their conversation." I kind of agreed with her, but I was dying to know what my dad and Penny were talking about, so I didn't say anything. And neither did Amanda, which was weird. Usually, whenever there was some kind of moral issue being debated, she was quick to jump on Traci's side of things. But not this time. I guess she was feeling pretty curious, too.

After a few seconds, Arielle crept back to the barn to give us a report.

"What did they say?" I asked, almost at the same time that Amanda said, "What did you hear?"

"Just more of what they were saying out here," Arielle replied, shaking her head. "She wants to make a donation to the shelter so he can hire some help, but he thinks it would be weird to have his girlfriend financing his work."

"Ooh, I guess it would be," I said. I hadn't really thought of it that way before. I guess I'd been too surprised by the fact that Penny had money to donate. I mean, all she does is baby-sit and have occasional art shows.

Arielle turned to Amanda. "Where's Penny planning to get the money to donate, anyway?" she asked. She always had the courage to say things I could only think.

Amanda shrugged. "I think she does pretty well with her artwork," she said. "Plus her parents died a few years ago, and I think they left her some money. At least, that's when she bought her house."

"Huh. I had no idea," Arielle said. I don't think any of us did, except maybe Amanda. Penny didn't exactly act like she had money to burn. She drove an old Volkswagen, dressed in hippie chic, and made most of her own jewelry.

"Well, anyway," Arielle went on, counting something off on her fingers. She ended on her pinky and looked up at us. "The timing's just about right."

"What do you mean?" Traci asked.

"I was just trying to figure out how long Penny and Mr. Fiol had been dating, and it's been about two months. That's about how long most of Penny's relationships last, isn't it, Amanda?"

"Arielle—how can you make jokes about this?" Amanda said, narrowing her eyes. "I, for one, don't think it's funny that Penny and Felicia's dad are fighting."

"Neither do I," I added quietly. But Arielle didn't look the least bit sorry about what she'd said. Instead she ran a hand through her hair and stared at us.

"I can't believe the two of you," she said. "You didn't want them to get together in the first place, and now you don't want them to break up."

"Who says they're breaking up?" Traci said. "All couples fight once in a while. It's normal."

"Nothing about Penny is normal," Arielle said.

"*Arielle*," Amanda warned her through gritted teeth. But it seemed to me that Arielle had a point.

"Okay, look," Arielle went on. "Forget what I said about Penny. The point isn't just that they're fighting. It's that they've only been together for two months or so and they're *already* fighting. They're still at the beginning of the relationship—this is supposed to be the easy part. Couples don't usually start fighting until they've been together long enough to have something real to fight about."

"That's the stupidest thing I've ever heard," Traci answered, shaking her head. She glanced at Amanda, but for the second time that afternoon Amanda didn't jump to back her up. In fact, she seemed to be considering what Arielle had just said. I know I was.

It wasn't like I was intent on getting my dad to break up with Penny anymore, but at the same time I knew that if they did it on their own, I wouldn't exactly be heartbroken. And from the look on Amanda's face, I didn't think she'd be too upset about it, either.

chapter
FIVE

PrincessA: RU out there FlowerGrl?

FlowerGrl: Right here. :-)

PrincessA: Have u gotten Felicia a birthday present yet?

FlowerGrl: No. U?

PrincessA: Nope. Any ideas?

FlowerGrl: I think I might draw something 4 her or paint her a picture.

PrincessA: EZ 4 u. I wish I was artistic.

FlowerGrl: U r!

PrincessA: Right. And ur preppy.

FlowerGrl: Funny. So what r u going 2 do?

PrincessA: I don't know. I'll come up with something.

FlowerGrl: I'm sure u will. C u tomorrow!

"I wish Mr. Reid had put us in the same group," Traci said, nibbling on one of her fries. It was Hot Off the Grill Day in the cafeteria, and they were serving garden burgers, hot dogs, barbecued chicken, and corn on the cob. It was actually a pretty good menu. There were even french fries, chips, and two kinds of salad.

"Me too," I agreed. "Who did you end up with?"

"Claudia, Heather T., Jeff, and Peter Watson," Traci said. "How about you?"

I closed my eyes and pictured the four people I'd been working with in math class. "Lauren, Sarah, James, and Ryan."

Traci sighed. "You're lucky," she said. "You have fun people in your group." She'd said *people*, but I knew there was one person in particular she was talking about: Ryan. "How long do you think we'll have to stay in these groups, anyway?" she asked.

"I think Mr. Reid said—"

"I'm glad you're here," Arielle interrupted suddenly. I hadn't even seen her and Amanda coming. "Did your dad say anything about Penny last night?" She set her tray down on the table and took the seat right next to mine while Amanda settled in across from her, next to Traci.

"Oh, hey—don't worry about interrupting us," Traci muttered. "Felicia and I can finish our conversation later."

Arielle flashed her a syrupy smile and said, "Thanks for understanding." Traci blew a stray strand of hair off her forehead. She was obviously annoyed, but Arielle ignored her and turned to me. "So anyway, Felicia," she went on. "Did he?"

48

Traci was fuming, but I had to laugh. Arielle's attitude cracks me up. Sure, she had been kind of rude, but Traci had sort of set herself up for that one.

"What? Say anything about Penny?" I asked. Arielle nodded. I shrugged. "No."

She seemed disappointed. "Not even after their dinner?"

"Actually, they didn't go. At about five-fifteen, Officer Smith stopped in with a stray dog, and Penny ended up leaving."

Arielle practically pounced on me. "What do you mean, she ended up leaving? Did she storm out? Did she yell? Did she *say* anything?"

"Not really," I said with a sigh.

Arielle frowned at me. "Come on, Felicia—this is important. Think. Did she and your dad say anything at all to each other before she went? Like, 'I'll talk to you later,' or anything like that? Or did she just leave?"

"I'm not sure," I said.

"Not everyone makes a habit of eavesdropping," Traci told Arielle, but Arielle just waved her off. She was focused on me—willing me to remember the details of last night. And I was trying. *Hard*. I was just about to give up when it came to me.

I sat up straight. "Actually, now that I think about it, she did say something—something about letting herself out since my dad had work to do." I was kind of proud of myself for coming up with it, but I have to say, it didn't seem like a big deal to me. Arielle, on the other hand, was gaping.

"Oh, my God—that's *huge*," she said.

"It is?" I asked. I exchanged a puzzled look with Amanda, who was on the other side of the table.

"Definitely," Arielle said. "Unless . . ." I could almost see the wheels turning in her head. "Did they call each other last night?" she asked.

I scrunched my eyebrows together. "I don't know. Maybe."

Again, Arielle looked frustrated with me. *"Maybe,"* she repeated. She sounded disgusted. "That's not good enough. We have to know for sure."

"Arielle, what's with all the questions?" Amanda asked. "You sound like you're using your lawyer voice to cross-examine Felicia."

"That's because I am," Arielle said.

"But why?" Amanda asked.

Arielle rolled her eyes. "Hello?" she said. "Am I the only one that remembers the fight Penny and Mr. Fiol had yesterday? It seemed pretty serious to me, and since two of the people at this table have a pretty strong interest in their relationship, I'm just trying to figure out *how* serious."

"Not this again," Traci muttered, stabbing a cherry tomato with her fork.

"If you're not interested, don't listen," Arielle advised her. I saw Traci look to Amanda for support, but

Amanda just kind of shrugged. Obviously, she was interested in what Arielle had to say. And so was I.

"So," Arielle continued, "in order to figure out just how important that fight was, we need to know if either one of them called to apologize last night." She turned to me. "Did they?"

"I don't think so," I said, replaying the previous night in my mind. "I know he called my mom to figure out what time she wanted me there on Friday, but aside from that, he was pretty busy with the new dog. He had to fill out a lot of forms and schedule the vet to come a day early. And after he got Pierre settled in—Pierre, that's what I'm calling the dog, he's this big black standard poodle that—"

"Felicia," Arielle stopped me. "The phone calls?"

"Oh, right," I said. "By the time he had Pierre down for the night, it was pretty late. So I don't think he really had a chance to call Penny. And every time the phone rang at our house, I answered it. So I know Penny didn't call him."

"That's what I figured," Arielle said. "I knew that fight was a big one." She looked from me to Amanda and back again. "This could be the end."

Traci exhaled so heavily that for a moment I thought she was choking. "Arielle—why are you making such a big deal out of this?" she asked. "We overheard one tiny argument between Penny and Mr. Fiol and you're turning it into this huge thing."

"I'm not turning it into a huge thing—it *is* a huge thing," Arielle corrected her.

"But . . . it was just one fight," Amanda said. "What makes you think they're going to break up over it?"

"Let's look at the facts," Arielle said. She was definitely in full lawyer mode now. I guess that's what happens when you grow up with two of them for parents. "First of all, none of us have ever thought that Penny and Mr. Fiol make a good match. They're way too different, right?"

I had to agree with that, and I knew Amanda did, too.

"But sometimes opposites attract," Traci argued.

"Maybe, but that's not the point," Arielle told her. "The point is that they're very different people, and that's what they were arguing about yesterday. Penny wants to buy Felicia's dad an assistant so he can spend more time with her, but Felicia's dad is too proud to let his girlfriend pay his way."

"*Arielle*," Amanda objected. "That's not why Penny offered to make a donation! She just wants to help out the shelter."

"*Maybe*, but—"

"And my dad's not too proud to accept donations," I added. "He's always happy to find more support for the shelter. He just likes to make sure he's doing things the right way."

Arielle rolled her eyes. "Okay," she said, "so maybe I didn't say that very well, but the thing is, they have different ways of doing things—and I'm not just talking about money issues, either. Your dad likes to plan things out and keep a schedule, right, Felicia?"

I pictured my dad's daily calendar, with every hour of every day filled in weeks ahead of time. "Definitely," I said.

"And Penny's way too—" Arielle stopped and looked at Amanda. I knew what she wanted to say. *Flighty. Spacey. Ditzy.* Or something like that. But that would have upset Amanda. "Um . . . free spirited?" Arielle tried. Amanda nodded. "Okay," Arielle went on, "so Penny's way too free spirited for him. She's not good at lists and schedules and all of that stuff, just like he's not good at taking a spontaneous idea—like Penny's offer to write a check—and running with it. He likes to think things through, but Penny's kind of . . ." Again she hesitated. "*Impulsive?*"

Amanda nodded her approval of the word. "Right, impulsive," Arielle said again. "And I think they're just starting to figure that out. The fight they had yesterday proves it."

"The *argument* that we overheard doesn't prove anything," Traci said.

"Maybe not by itself," Arielle agreed. "But don't forget—they canceled their dinner plans and didn't even bother to call each other to talk about it later. Plus Penny made that comment about Mr. Fiol having work to do before she walked out. Did they even say good-bye to each other, Felicia?"

"I don't think so," I admitted. It seemed to me that Arielle was building a pretty strong case.

"That doesn't mean anything," Traci said. "Maybe Penny rushed out because of Pierre. Felicia said he was a big dog, and she *is* still scared of them."

"But if that was why she walked out, then why didn't she wait in her car for Mr. Fiol so they could still have dinner? Or at least call him to reschedule." Amanda and I both nodded. It was a good point. Even Traci seemed to be considering that one.

"Nope," Arielle went on. "I don't think the dog had anything to do with it. I think this is the beginning of the end. Penny needs someone more . . . uh, *free spirited*, and Mr. Fiol needs someone more organized. Like your mom, Felicia. I mean, I know they're divorced and everything, but they were together for a long time, right?"

"Fifteen years," I said. "And they never fought. In fact, just this weekend my mom and I were talking about how nice it was when we were all together on our family vacations." Arielle's mouth dropped open, and she stared at me. "What?" I asked.

"Felicia," she said. "I can't believe you didn't tell me that before. Now it all *really* makes sense."

"What do you mean?" I looked at Amanda and Traci, but they seemed just as confused as I was.

"*Your parents*," Arielle said. "Isn't it obvious? They miss each other."

"They what?" I asked.

"They miss each other," she repeated.

"Oh, come on, Arielle. How do you know that?" Traci demanded. "Are you psychic or something?"

"*No-o*, but I can put a few facts together to figure something out," Arielle responded.

"What facts?" Traci asked.

"Number one," Arielle said, holding out her index finger. "Felicia's mom practically came right out and said it."

I could almost hear my mother's voice. *Those were fun times*, she had said. And she had seemed so sad.

"Number two," Arielle went on, ticking off another finger. "In all the time they've been apart, neither one of them has done any serious dating. Number three: It only took Felicia's dad a couple of months to realize that the first person he'd decided to date was all wrong for him. And number four: When he had a fight with Penny—who did he call?"

"My mom," I said. "He called my mom." It hadn't occurred to me before, but he had been on the phone with her for a pretty long time. A lot longer than it takes to decide what time to drop me off.

I looked over at Amanda, who raised her eyebrows slightly, as if to ask me what I thought. And what I thought was that for about the fortieth time during that lunch period, Arielle had made a good point. But Traci wasn't convinced.

"I don't know," she said. "I still think you're making

a major leap. This is all based on . . ." She bit her lip. "What do you call it when there are a lot of facts in a case but no real proof?"

"Circumstantial evidence?" Arielle guessed.

"Yeah, that's it—circumstantial evidence," Traci repeated.

Arielle shrugged. "Sometimes that's all you need," she said. Traci groaned. "But if you want proof," Arielle added quickly, "I know how you can get it."

"How?" I asked. I wasn't sure I bought the whole idea of my parents missing each other. It did seem kind of far-fetched—especially considering that they'd been apart for two years now. But I had to admit that some of the stuff Arielle had said seemed to make sense.

"Easy," Arielle said. "You just get them some time alone together and see what happens."

chapter
SIX

Dear Diary—

I wonder if Arielle could be right. What if my parents really do miss each other? What if they are just beginning to feel like they've made a big mistake? If they were Arielle's parents, she wouldn't just sit back and wonder. She'd do something about it. She'd get them alone together, like she said. But how?

"Come on, Pierre," I said. "You need to get back in your kennel now." I took hold of the thick red collar my dad had given him and guided him back toward his cage. He went in easily, unlike most of the other dogs, who practically had to be pushed.

"Now, there's one that's already had some obedience training," my father said. I jumped at the sound of his voice.

"Dad," I breathed. "I thought you were still in the office."

"I'm sorry—did I scare you?" he asked.

"Only a little," I said. "I guess I didn't hear you come out."

"Ah. Probably because I went out the front door

and walked over by the duck pond first. I finished all of my paperwork and phone calls early for once," he said. "So I actually had a chance to take my time and enjoy going the long way around."

"Oh," I said, trying to picture my dad strolling past the duck pond, taking his time. He's usually in such a hurry. It was kind of hard to imagine him *strolling* anywhere.

I gave Pierre one last pat behind the ears and latched his cage. "There you go, boy," I said. "Sleep well tonight." He sniffed my hand through the metal wire, licked me once, then went and curled up on his bed.

"I guess you're right," I told my dad. "He does look like he's had some obedience training."

"Mm-hmm." My father nodded. "Or it could be that he's just old enough to have mellowed out a bit by now."

"How old do you think he is?" I asked.

"Well, when the vet stopped by today to check him out, he said he could be nine or ten."

"Wow," I said. "That's pretty old for a dog."

"Yeah, it is," my father agreed.

"Especially a stray," I added. I'd learned by now that animals living on the street didn't usually live as long as ones with permanent homes.

"That's the thing," my father said. "I don't think Pierre is a stray."

"Why not?"

"Well, when Dr. Allen examined him this afternoon, he mentioned how soft Pierre's paw pads are—not like the feet of an animal that's been living on the street for a long time. Plus, he's fairly well-groomed. Poodles don't shed, but Pierre's fur isn't terribly long, which means he was probably clipped within the last month or so. I think someone's actually been taking good care of him—at least up until a few days ago."

I scrunched up my face. "I don't get it," I said. "If someone's been taking such good care of him, why did they suddenly abandon him?"

"That's just it. I'm not sure he *was* abandoned—maybe just lost. It wouldn't surprise me if someone came in to claim this one."

"That would be nice," I said. My father nodded. So many of the animals were in bad shape by the time they got to us. It would be good to see one who came from a decent home for once. "But then again . . ." I started, an idea suddenly coming to me.

"What?"

"*Well* . . . I was just thinking—Pierre's such a gentle dog, he might be a good one to have Penny meet. You know, to help get her used to bigger dogs?" It was a stretch, I knew. I wasn't exactly in the habit of coming up with friendly suggestions for spending time with Penny. But I wanted to see how my dad would react to her name.

He narrowed his eyes, but not at me. "I don't

know," he said, looking doubtful. "I don't think Pierre's going to be here very long. If his owner doesn't come for him, someone else will adopt him pretty quickly. He's a good dog."

I stared at my father, who was staring at Pierre. I couldn't believe it. Not only had he *not* jumped at the chance to get Penny over here to bond with me, but he hadn't questioned the reason for my suggestion at all, either. He hadn't even given me the suspicious look I deserved.

Instead he'd just stared off into space—or maybe into Pierre. But either way it didn't seem like a normal reaction to me. And taking the long way around to the backyard was totally out of character for him, too.

So at least one thing was clear—my dad wasn't acting like his usual self. And after everything Arielle had said at lunch, I could only think of one reason for him to be behaving so strangely. His fight with Penny must have been a serious one. Maybe even serious enough for them to have broken up.

"Felicia!"

I was sitting on my bed that night, writing in my diary, when my dad knocked on my bedroom door.

"Come in." I closed my diary and placed it carefully on my nightstand. I always like to write in my diary before I go to sleep. It helps me sort of let go of the day and get ready for a new one.

My dad opened the door and held out our cordless phone, smiling. "Phone for you. Remember to make it quick. It's getting late."

I grabbed the phone and nodded. "Okay, Dad. Ten minutes, I promise."

He walked out and closed the door behind him as I held the phone up to my ear. "Hello?"

"Hey, Feleesh, what's up?" I was ready for bed, but Arielle sounded all bouncy and energized on the other end of the line.

"Oh, hey, Arielle. Not much here. What's up with you?"

Arielle gave a dismissive snort. "Nothing. I'm totally bored over here. My dad's working way late, and my mom's down in the kitchen paying bills. So, did your dad say anything else?"

I had to think a minute to figure out what she was getting at. "Oh, about my mom?"

"Of *course* about your mom."

I frowned. "Well . . . not really."

"Not really?" I could hear Arielle perk up. "Does that mean he *sort of* said something?"

"Well . . ." I felt kind of funny even mentioning this to Arielle. The truth was, my dad might have said it for any reason. "I was taking care of Pierre today— you know, the French poodle that came in yesterday? And I said maybe he would be a good dog for Penny to spend time with because he's really gentle."

"Yeah?" I could hear the excitement in Arielle's voice.

"But then my dad seemed totally against it. He just said, 'Oh, I think Pierre will be adopted soon, he's such a good dog.' He totally tried to change the subject!"

"Aha!" cried Arielle. "You see? He doesn't want to talk about Penny because they had that big fight and he thinks things are over. This is definitely the right time to get him and your mom together!"

"You think?" I rested my pinky finger between my lips and started biting on it. Arielle was saying exactly what I wanted to hear, but something about it made me nervous.

"Absolutely!" I could hear Arielle getting up and shifting on her big canopy bed. "See, adults are *so* predictable. He and Penny were just never right for each other."

"That's what I thought," I agreed. Just as I was about to say something else, I heard a loud *beep* on the phone. At first I thought I had hit one of the numbers, but then I remembered our call-waiting. Someone was on the other line. My heart thumped. What if it was my mom, wanting to talk to my dad?

"Hey, um, Arielle, can you hold on a minute?" I didn't even wait for her answer. I pressed a button on the top of the keypad and switched over to the other caller. "Hello?"

"Felicia?"

It took me a minute to recognize the voice on the line because I had been positive it was my mom. "Patrick?"

"Hey, I know it's late, I just wanted to ask you a question."

"Oh—sure, Patrick. Can you hold on a minute?"

"Okay."

I pressed the button again and clicked back over to Arielle. She was humming a Shauna Ferris song, and I could hear her drumming on her bed.

"Arielle?"

"Oh, hey, Feleesh. So, anyway, I think what we need to do now is get your mom and dad in the same room together. Like, maybe—"

"Um, Arielle? Actually, I have to go. I have to get off the phone in a couple of minutes, and I have—" I paused. How to say this? I didn't want Arielle to think I was putting Patrick ahead of her, though I sort of was. Why did she have to call right before bedtime? "I, um, have an urgent call on the other line."

"An *urgent* call? Oh, sure. No problem. Is it your mom?"

"Um, no." I picked at the threads in my quilt. "Actually, it's Patrick."

"Oh." That's all Arielle said. There wasn't even any drumming, singing, or shifting around on her bed in the background.

I felt really, really bad.

"So, I'll talk to you at school tomorrow, okay?"

"Sure." I could hear a mattress squeaking like Arielle was sitting up to put the phone back. "All right, then. Later."

And then she hung up.

I didn't have time to get worried about it, though. I had to hear Patrick's question before it was time for me to go to bed. "Patrick?" I asked, clicking over.

"Hey, Felicia. I was just wondering, want to go to the arcade tomorrow after school? I thought we could have a rematch on Alien Annihilators. I think I can beat you this time."

I had to smile in spite of myself. The week before, Patrick had challenged me on my favorite video game, Alien Annihilators. Of course, I had beat the pants off him. But he was so fun to be with—really funny and nice.

"All right, Patrick. But I wouldn't be too sure about beating me. I got you pretty bad last time."

"Yeah, yeah, yeah." I could almost hear the smile in Patrick's voice. "But I've been practicing, see, and there's no way a *girl* could beat me now."

I laughed. "Oh, is that how it is?"

"Felicia!" Suddenly, I heard my dad's voice just outside my room. "It's been fifteen minutes now! Time for bed."

"All right, Dad," I called. I turned back to the phone. "Hey, I've got to go. But you're on for tomorrow. In

fact, you might want to try and get in a few more practice sessions."

Patrick chuckled. "Maybe I will. See you tomorrow."

"Bye."

I clicked off the phone and stood up to bring it back
to the kitchen. I had two really strong, really different
feelings: guilt for kind of blowing off Arielle and
excitement at getting to spend time with Patrick again.

Having best friends and a guy friend isn't always
easy.

On my way out of lunch on Wednesday, I realized
that I'd been thinking about getting my parents back
together for nearly twenty-four hours straight. I'd
even thought about it in my sleep.

I had this dream that my parents stood up at my
birthday party and announced that they were getting
back together. It had seemed so real that for a
moment after I woke up, I still believed it had actually happened. But then, after I rubbed my eyes and
glanced around my room, I realized that it was only
Wednesday, and I hadn't even had my birthday party
yet. Boy, was I disappointed.

So anyway, I hadn't really been able to focus on
anything else—which is probably why I hadn't been
able to answer Mr. Reid the two times he called on
me in math class. And why I hadn't been able to
remember the Spanish word for *supermarket* even

though Arielle was whispering the answer to me from the next row over. And it's probably also why I didn't notice Brian McFee coming down the hall toward me, Traci, and Arielle when we were on our way to our lockers after school.

At least, I *hadn't* noticed him. Until Traci elbowed Arielle in the ribs so hard that she fell into me and almost knocked me over.

"Ow," Arielle said. "What was that about?"

"Here's your chance," Traci whispered to Arielle. "He's all alone. Ask him to come to Felicia's party."

After I recovered from being knocked off balance, I glanced up to see Brian. He was only a few feet away. I sucked in my breath and looked at Arielle to see what she was going to do. What I saw surprised me. She actually looked scared. At least, I thought she did.

But it was hard to tell. Because half a second later she had a big grin on her face and she was giving Brian a superflirty look. "Hi, Brian," she said in a voice I only ever heard her use when she was talking to guys. Cute ones, anyway.

"Hey, Arielle," he said, smiling back. Then he glanced at me and Traci and nodded as he walked by, which I thought was kind of cool. I hadn't expected him to know our names, but it was nice that he didn't just ignore us.

"Wow—he is *so* cute," I said when we were around the corner.

"You can say that again," Arielle agreed.

"So why didn't you ask him?" Traci said. "That was a perfect opportunity."

"Oh, yeah," Arielle said. "With you right there jabbing me in the ribs? I don't think so."

"What's going on?" Amanda asked as she jogged to catch up with us. She'd been in the library doing research for a student council presentation she was helping with.

"Arielle just chickened out," Traci told her.

Amanda scrunched up her face and looked at Arielle.

"Apparently in South Carolina it's considered good luck to bodycheck your friends whenever a cute guy is approaching," Arielle sneered, glaring at Traci.

"What are you guys talking about?" Amanda asked. She glanced to me for an explanation.

"We just passed Brian McFee," I said. "And Traci thinks Arielle should have invited him to my party."

"Oh," Amanda said. "Well—why didn't you?"

Arielle clicked her tongue. "Because for one thing, I prefer to do that kind of stuff one-on-one—not with an audience," she said, focusing on Traci. "That would be totally lame. It would be like I didn't dare to talk to him without my friends around or something."

Personally, I needed all the support I could get when it came to stuff like that. But I could see Arielle's point.

"And second, I haven't actually made up my mind if I'm going to invite him yet."

"But I thought—" I started, remembering what Arielle had said in Spanish class on Monday.

"You thought *what?*" Arielle said, training her green eyes on me. I wasn't sure, but I kind of got the feeling that she didn't want me to say anything. So I didn't.

"Nothing," I said, chewing on my fingernail.

"The party's only two days away," Traci said to Arielle. "You better make up your mind soon."

"I will," Arielle said. "But right now I've got other things to think about."

"Like what?" Traci asked.

"Like macaroons," Arielle said with a grin. Traci and I just stared at each other, but Amanda's face lit up.

"Did Anya make some today?" she asked, practically licking her lips.

"Mm-hmm." Arielle nodded.

Amanda turned to me and Traci. "Arielle's housekeeper, Anya, makes the most incredible macaroons. They're these little flower-shaped chocolate cookies, and she sticks chunks of white chocolate and candied cherries on the top."

"Wow, they sound great," Traci said. She had that same look in her eyes she'd had the other night when my mom brought out the brownies.

"Anyone want to come over and have some?" Arielle asked.

"I'd love to," Traci said, "but I can't today. I'm helping out at the shelter."

"Again?" Arielle asked.

"Sure," Traci said with a shrug. "I love volunteering there."

"Uh-huh. And Ryan will be there for Lola's obedience lesson, too. Won't he?" Arielle said. "How convenient."

Traci's face went red. Busted. I mean, sure, she loves the animals, but it was obvious they weren't the only reason she was going.

Next, Arielle turned to Amanda. "How about you?"

"I wish I could," Amanda said, "but Penny's picking me up so we can go over to the new skate park today."

"Skate park?" Arielle sneered. "That's weird even for Penny."

Amanda put her hands on her hips. "It's not weird. The Wonder Lake town council asked her to create some art for the park to spruce it up a bit. So she's going to check it out, and I told her I'd help."

"A sculpture or something out there would be cool," Traci said. "It's so boring the way it is now."

"You've been to the skate park?" I asked. Traci was athletic, but I had no idea she was into skateboarding.

"Just to pick up Dave with my mom," Traci explained. "He's been out there practically every day after school since it opened."

"Oh, really," Arielle said, cocking her head at Amanda.

Of course, we had reached Amanda's locker by that time, so she was pretending to be busy with the lock. "Gee," she said, without meeting Arielle's gaze. "That's funny. I had no idea Dave liked to go there."

"Yeah, right," Arielle jeered. "Strike two. Well, Felicia," she went on, turning her attention to me. "That leaves you and me. I guess there will just be more macaroons for us."

Boy, did I feel horrible. Especially after the excuses Traci and Amanda had just offered up. But what else could I do? "Um, I'd really like to, but . . ." The weight of her eyes was almost too much.

"What? Are you going to the skate park, too?" Arielle asked.

"No," I said. "The arcade."

"*Alone?*"

"No . . . with Patrick," I said quietly.

"Oh," Arielle said. She gave each of us a kind of disappointed scowl, then shrugged. "Well, your loss. I better get going before I miss the bus." She walked hurriedly toward her locker and began stuffing books in her bag. Then, without a second look back at us, she headed down the hall.

"Do you think she's okay?" I asked Traci and Amanda.

"Sure," said Traci. "Why wouldn't she be?"

"I don't know," I said. "I just thought that maybe, well—the *guy* thing might be bothering her."

"What guy thing?" Traci asked.

"You know," I said. "The fact that we all have . . . well, *guys*. And she doesn't."

"I don't think so," Amanda answered, shaking her head. "She hasn't said anything to me about it, and if she was upset, she would."

"Yeah, and besides, she's having way too much fun teasing us," Traci added. "If she had a crush, she wouldn't be able to."

I nodded, but I wasn't so sure. If I were in Arielle's position, I'd feel really left out. Of course, I'm not Arielle. Not by a long shot. And if Traci and Amanda weren't concerned, there was probably no reason for me to be. Amanda had known Arielle since before kindergarten. If Arielle was upset, she'd know. Wouldn't she?

chapter
SEVEN

From the Desk of Arielle Davis

<u>Reasons I'm Glad I Don't Have a Boyfriend</u>

1. Boys can be so immature. Like Ryan Bradley and his cafeteria food fights—I don't know what Traci sees in him.
2. They take up way too much time. As if I'd want to waste my afternoon at an arcade when I could be shopping.
3. They have stupid hobbies. Skateboarding? Hello? It's a piece of wood with wheels. Doesn't that get old after a while?
4. Traci was right—all couples fight once in a while, and who needs that?
5. I don't have to stick with just one guy all the time. I can invite someone to Felicia's party this week and then hang out with someone else next week.

"It's so cool that you like Alien Annihilators," Patrick said as we each put one more token into the machine. "Most girls don't."

"Really? Why not?" I asked.

"I don't know. My mom and my sister say there's too much killing."

"Well, it is pretty violent," I said. "But I just pretend that all the aliens are sick animals and that I'm giving them vaccinations."

Patrick frowned in a puzzled way. He looked really cute when he did that. "Are you serious?" he asked.

"Yeah," I said.

"Vaccinations? With a gun?"

I reached forward and grabbed my joystick. It was shaped like a rifle, so I had to use both hands. "It's not a gun," I told him. "It's a long-range hypodermic syringe." I knew Patrick was smiling at me. I could see him out of the corner of my eye. It made my heart speed up, and I felt kind of nervous but in a nice way. Still, I didn't want to say or do anything stupid, so I pushed the red START GAME button.

"Whoa—hold on," Patrick called. He grabbed his joystick, and within seconds we were blasting away, shoulder to shoulder.

When we had finished, I glanced at our scores. I had beaten Patrick by nearly three thousand points.

"Jeez, I guess your 'save the animals' strategy really works," he said. "Maybe I should give it a try."

"I don't know why they don't make video games like that, anyway," I said. "It's a lot more fun to save things than to blast them."

Patrick smirked. "I kind of like the blasting," he said, and we both laughed. "But don't tell my mom I said that. Or my sister," he added. "My father, on the other hand . . ."

"Does he like video games?"

"Yeah," Patrick said as we walked out of the arcade and into the mall. "Sometimes he plays them with me when I'm over at his house."

"Even the violent ones?" I asked.

"Uh-huh. *Well*—at least now he does. When I was younger, he'd only let me get games like car racing or golf."

"What about at your mom's house?"

"She's not too bad. She lets me get games where you have to find clues to solve mysteries. And they can be kind of violent sometimes, too—you know, with murders and stuff. But she says that at least I have to use my brain for those—it's not just pointing and shooting."

I laughed. That's all Alien Annihilators was— pointing and shooting. Which is why I preferred to think of it as pointing and vaccinating. At least then there seemed to be some kind of purpose.

"It must be weird having different rules at each house," I said.

"Your parents are divorced, too," Patrick said. "Isn't it like that for you?"

"Kind of. I guess. But . . . actually, I don't know. It seems like my parents have pretty much the same rules. I can't think of anything that's really different."

"Nothing?" Patrick asked.

I thought it over. Homework before TV or computer, no phone calls after nine. Bedtime at nine-thirty on school nights. Help with the chores around the house. "Nope. Not that I can think of."

"Hmmm. That's pretty cool, I guess. They must be a lot alike."

"They are." I nodded, and all at once everything Arielle had said about them missing each other came flooding into my mind again. "In fact," I started, but I wasn't sure if I should tell him about it. "Actually . . . never mind."

"What?" Patrick asked.

"Well . . ." I studied his brown eyes, which seemed to be studying mine. We'd only known each other for a few weeks, but already I felt really comfortable around him. At least, I did when my heart wasn't pounding sixty beats per second because of the way he smiled at me. But I could trust him with this. I knew I could.

"It's just that . . . yesterday at lunch my friends and I were talking, and I kind of realized that . . . well, that my parents seem to, I don't know . . . *miss* each other."

"What do you mean?"

"Well, for one thing, it's been two years since they got divorced, and neither one of them has really dated anybody else." I decided to leave Penny out of the picture. After that fight she and my dad had, she didn't seem that important anymore, anyway. "Plus they talk a lot on the phone. And they get along really well—they never fight or even disagree about stuff."

"Yeah, but that doesn't mean—"

"And my mom told me straight out that she misses my dad," I blurted.

Patrick stopped. We'd made it as far as the ice-cream shop in the center of the mall. "She said that?"

"Well—not exactly," I had to admit. "But that's what she meant," I added. Why didn't the facts sound as convincing coming from me as they had from Arielle? I must be leaving something out.

"Huh. Well, maybe they do miss each other," Patrick said finally. I couldn't tell if he meant it or if he was just going along with me because it was easier.

"Do you really think so?" I asked.

"Sure. I mean, they were together for a long time, right?"

"Fifteen years."

"So it makes sense that they'd miss each other a little. You get used to having people around after a while."

I sighed. "Yeah, but I think it's more than that—more

than just missing someone because you're used to having them around."

"What are you saying?"

"I think they *really* miss each other," I said. "Like, maybe they wish they were back together."

Patrick stared at me. "Hold on a second," he said. "You don't actually think that your parents are going to get back together—do you?"

"I don't know," I said with a shrug. I was thinking *yes*, but something about the way he was squinting sideways at me told me that might not go over so well. "Maybe," I answered instead.

Patrick frowned. "Uh-uh. You can't start hoping for that—it's pointless."

"Why?"

"Because. It is. It's what every kid whose parents get divorced thinks is going to happen, but most of the time it doesn't."

"That means some of the time it does," I said.

"Yeah, but not often," Patrick said. "Trust me. I used to want my parents to get back together, and it was hard when they didn't. But then I finally realized that it just wasn't going to happen, and you know what? Now I think they're both a lot happier apart. My dad's remarried, and my mom's seeing this guy who seems pretty cool, and—"

"But my parents aren't seeing other people," I said.

"*Really?* I thought your dad had a girlfriend. That

woman you didn't really like all that much—what was her name?"

I was surprised Patrick remembered her. I'd only complained about her once. Or maybe twice. "Penny," I said. "But he's not seeing her anymore." At least, he hadn't said a word about her since that fight they had on Monday, and that was good enough for me.

Patrick was eyeing me sideways again. "Since when?"

I stared down at my feet. I wasn't about to tell him it had only been two days. He already seemed to be having a hard time accepting my theory. I wished Arielle was there to back me up.

"That's not important," I said, without looking up at him. "But the *reason* they broke up is."

"Oh, yeah?"

"Yeah," I said, feeling a little more confident now that I'd remembered this part of Arielle's argument. I looked directly into Patrick's eyes. "They broke up because she's nothing like my mom," I told him. But instead of being impressed, Patrick was watching me with something like pity in his eyes.

"I'm serious," I said. "Penny was way too flighty and flaky, and my dad needs someone more . . . *normal*. And organized, like he is." I waited, but Patrick's expression didn't change. "And do you know who he called as soon as he and Penny split?" I said. "My mom." That should have sealed it, but Patrick didn't budge.

"Felicia, I know you really want things to be like they used to be, but—"

"But what?" I snapped. I was getting really annoyed with the way he kept questioning everything I said. Why couldn't he just believe me?

"I just think you might be overreacting. You need to—"

"I don't need to do anything," I snapped, surprised by my tone of voice. I guess I was more upset than I had realized.

"Hey—I'm not trying to make you mad. I just don't think you should get your hopes up. I know when I used to wish that my parents would—"

"We're not talking about your parents," I told him. "We're talking about mine."

"Still, I—"

"You know what? Forget it. Just forget I even brought it up. I should have known you wouldn't get it."

"Felicia," he said. I looked up at him for a minute. The expression in his eyes wasn't angry or upset, even though I'd practically blown up at him. He still looked like he just felt sorry for me. It was more than I could take.

"I have to get home," I said, turning around. And before he could say anything else, I stormed away. I didn't need to hear any more of his arguments. Or maybe I just didn't want to.

Later I was sitting in my room when the phone rang. I almost didn't answer it because I figured it would probably be Patrick, and I definitely wasn't in the mood for more questions. Then again, if I didn't answer, I wouldn't know if it was Penny or not without asking my dad. And I definitely didn't want to get him thinking about her when he wasn't. So I picked up.

"Hello?"

"Hi, Felicia, it's Amanda."

"Oh, hi," I said, breathing a sigh of relief. "What's up?"

"Not much. I just thought I'd call to say hi and see what you were up to."

"Oh," I said, kind of caught off guard. Amanda had never called me just to chat before. At least, I didn't think she had. It seemed like she always had a reason for calling. I glanced at my math book, which was lying open on my desk. "I'm just doing home-work," I said. "You?"

Amanda sighed. "Trying to make sense of all of this information I got in the library today."

"What sort of information?" I asked.

"School budgets, mostly. *Three hundred pages of school budgets*."

"Wow," I said. "That's a lot."

"Yeah, and it just looks like a bunch of numbers to me right now," Amanda said. "But Asher wants me to figure out how much the Wonder Lake school district has been spending on sports versus arts over the last five years so we can use it for our presentation to the school board."

Asher Banks is the president of the WLMS student government, and Amanda was just elected as our sixth-grade class president, but she wasn't wasting any time. She had gotten involved in the debate about cutting arts funding to the school right away, and it seemed like Asher was counting on her to do a lot of the legwork for their argument as to why it shouldn't be cut.

"Jeez," I said. "Going through all that stuff must take a long time."

"It does," Amanda said. "But it will be worth it if it convinces the school board not to cut arts funding."

"Yeah. I guess it will," I agreed. Amanda's so cool like that. If she finds a cause she believes in, she jumps right in. And no matter what Arielle says, I know she didn't join the student government just because Asher is so cute. She joined because she really wants to make a difference, and I know she will. She's such a positive person. I guess you could say that Amanda has really good energy, too.

"So," Amanda said after a moment of silence. I waited a minute, but she didn't add anything else. I sort of felt like she was waiting for me to say something, but I wasn't sure what.

"So," I echoed. "Um . . . how was the skate park?"

"Oh. It was okay. But Traci's right. It is kind of boring looking out there. Just a lot of concrete and metal. Penny's artwork will really help."

"That's good," I said. And then it was quiet again. I was beginning to feel kind of worried that maybe she'd realized I wasn't very interesting to talk to one-on-one.

"So, anyway," she said after what seemed like forever, "can you believe Arielle?"

I pressed my eyebrows together. Was I supposed to know what she was talking about? "You mean because she doesn't know who she's inviting to my party yet?" I guessed.

"Actually, I was thinking about all that stuff she said at lunch yesterday. You know, about Penny and your dad. I mean, she has some crazy theories, doesn't she?"

"Oh, *that*," I said. "Yeah. I guess she does."

"Not that it was totally far-fetched or anything," Amanda added quickly. "At least, *I* didn't think it was. Did you?"

"What? Think that it was far-fetched?" I asked.

"Yeah," she said. "That stuff about Penny and your dad being a bad match and your parents missing each other—I mean, what did you think of all that?"

"I don't know," I said. "I guess I haven't thought about it too much." That was a lie, but after my fight with Patrick, I wasn't exactly dying to tell anyone else that I thought Arielle was right. Not even one of my best friends.

"Oh," she said, sounding kind of disappointed. "Because I kind of thought . . . well . . . actually, never mind," she finished, but I could tell she wanted to say more.

"What?" I asked.

"It's just that . . . I don't know. I guess I sort of thought she had some good points."

"You *did?*"

"Well, yeah. I mean, I've never really thought of Penny and your dad as a perfect couple, have you?"

"Uh-uh," I said. I couldn't think of anyone that could be any *less* perfect for my dad.

"And it seemed like you thought that maybe she was right about your parents missing each other," she went on.

"Yeah, I do think that," I admitted.

"Really? That's great," Amanda said. "Not that it matters to me or anything, but . . . well, you know."

Yeah, I did know. And suddenly, Amanda's phone call was making a lot more sense to me. If my dad and Penny broke up, Penny would have more time to spend with Amanda again. And she'd stop making such a big deal about me all the time just to get on my dad's good side, which meant Amanda would have her full attention again, too.

"So, then . . . have you thought about what she said about getting your parents alone together?" Amanda asked. She was still trying to sound casual, but I knew what she was thinking now. If my mom and dad got back together, that would guarantee that

Penny and my dad were done for good. But I didn't care what Amanda's motives were. I was just glad to have another ally. Especially since Patrick thought the whole idea of my parents getting back together again was ridiculous.

"I've thought about it," I said, "but I'm not sure how to do it."

"Yeah, that's a tough one," Amanda agreed. "Maybe Arielle has some ideas."

Arielle! It was so obvious—why hadn't I thought of it before? "I bet you're right," I said. "Thanks, Amanda."

"Thanks?" she said. "For what?"

"For calling," I told her. After my afternoon with Patrick, I'd started doubting myself, but now I was feeling hopeful about the whole situation again. For one thing, Amanda had let me know that I wasn't the only one who thought Arielle was right. But more important, she'd made me realize that I needed to do something about it—and now I knew what.

chapter
EIGHT

Instant Messages from FiFiol to PrincessA

FiFiol: How were the macaroons?

PrincessA: Awesome. 2 bad u missed it.

FiFiol: Yeah. Maybe next time.

PrincessA: Definitely.

FiFiol: Hey, I've been thinking . . . if I wanted 2 get my parents alone together, like u said, how would I do it?

PrincessA: EZ. Get yr dad 2 help with yr party. They'll have 2 meet 2 plan stuff.

FiFiol: Good idea. But how do I get him 2 help?

PrincessA: Even EZ-er. Tell yr mom that yr dad wants 2 b involved. Then tell yr dad yr mom needs some help. They'll do the rest.

FiFiol: Do u really think that will work?

PrincessA: I know it will. Trust me. If they hesitate at all, give them yr

best smile and tell them it would
mean a lot 2 u. That always does
it. 'Rents r sooo predictable.

"Hello?"

"Uh, hi—*Mom?*" I said.

She laughed. "Who else would it be?" She had a good point. I had called *her* house.

"I don't know," I said, realizing just how nervous I was about putting Arielle's plan into action. I'd never really lied to my mom about anything before, and even though it wasn't a big lie, I felt kind of funny about it. I was gripping the phone so tight that my hand was getting all sweaty.

"Felicia? Was there something you wanted to talk about?" my mom asked after a moment.

"Oh, yeah," I said. "Um, I was just wondering how everything's going for my party on Friday night."

"Everything's going just fine," my mom said. "But I'm not giving you any hints about your birthday presents."

I clicked my tongue. "I *know*," I said. "That's not why I called."

"No?" my mother questioned. I don't think she believed me, but that was okay. As long as she didn't know what I was really up to.

"No," I said. "I just wanted to see if you needed any help with anything."

"Oh. Well, that's nice of you, honey, but you shouldn't have to help out with your own birthday party. I can take care of it."

"Actually, I sort of thought that maybe Dad could help you out," I said.

"Your father?" my mother asked.

"Yeah."

"And just when did he put you in charge of coordinating his volunteer activities?" she asked.

I sighed. "He didn't," I told her. "He was just talking about the party at dinner last night, and I kind of got the feeling that he wished he could be more involved."

"Did he *say* that?" my mother asked. She was beginning to sound suspicious. I could almost see her standing in the middle of her kitchen with her head cocked and her hand on her hip.

"Well, no," I admitted, "not exactly. It's just that . . ." I let my voice trail off. I wasn't sure exactly how far I should go to convince her that he wanted to help out.

"It's just what?"

Oh, boy, I thought. She definitely wasn't making things easy for me. It looked like I was going to have to come right out and lie. *But it's for a good cause*, I told myself. After all, if my parents ever came to me and told me that they wanted to get back together, I wouldn't stand in their way. So what was wrong with giving them a little nudge?

I took a deep breath. It was now or never. "Well . . . he was just talking about how this would be the first year ever that he wouldn't be at my party or helping to plan it or anything, and he sounded kind of sad."

"*Really?*" my mother asked.

"Yeah. I mean, not like he was super-upset about it or anything, but . . . I don't know. I just got the feeling he wanted to be part of it."

My mother was silent for a moment, which was a good sign. If she'd thought I was making things up, she would have jumped on me right away. Instead I had her thinking. "But I thought he and Penny were doing something special with you on Friday afternoon," she said finally.

That would be one *way to ruin my birthday*, I thought. "Well, he hasn't said anything to me about it," I said. "And besides, he and Penny had a big fight. I don't think they're even talking."

"Oh, no," my mom said. "That's too bad." But she didn't sound too broken up about it, as far as I could tell. "Well, I certainly don't mind if he helps. It might be kind of nice to have someone else taking care of the little details—like decorations. That way I can concentrate on the cake and the rest of the food. And I guess it will be nice for you to have everyone in one place for your birthday," she added, and I couldn't have agreed more.

It was going to be nice to have my family back in one place. Period.

*   *   *

"How was your day?" my dad asked as he heaped a spoonful of peas onto his plate.

"Okay," I said. I speared a drumstick from the platter of chicken in front of me. They were my favorite pieces, and my dad knew it. He always left me both of them.

"What did you do in school today?" he asked.

"Noth—" I started, but I caught myself. Dad hated it when I said "nothing." He always told me that if I couldn't give him at least one decent answer to that question, then either I wasn't trying hard enough or my teachers weren't, in which case he'd need to have a talk with them. And since I really didn't want him to do that, I always tried to come up with something.

But the problem was, I didn't want to talk about school. I wanted to talk about my party and convince my father that my mother needed help with it. Still, I couldn't just jump into that without answering his question first. I thought for a minute. "Oh, I know. In English class we had a mock spelling bee."

"Yeah? And how did you do?" my dad asked.

"Not too good," I said, curling my lip.

"Not too *well*," he corrected me. "What word got you?"

"*Separate*," I said. "I spelled it *s-e-p*-e-*r-a-t-e*, and it's supposed to be *s-e-p*-a-*r-a-t-e*."

"That's a tough one." My dad nodded as he cut up his chicken. "Do you know how you can remember that?" he asked. It was just like him. He always had little tips and tricks for remembering everything.

"No. How?" I said.

"Think of it this way: Separate has *a rat* in the middle of it," he said, popping a piece of chicken into his mouth.

I thought it over. *A rat?* "Oh, I get it," I said. "A rat. As in *a-r-a-t*. That's pretty cool, Dad."

"My sixth-grade teacher taught me that," he said with a grin. "Her name was Mrs. Bishop, and she was a really good teacher. But then I guess she must have been if I still remember her thirty years later."

"Wow," I said. "Thirty years."

"It's not that long." My father chuckled. "Besides, you're getting up there yourself, you know. You'll be twelve years old on Friday."

I grinned, and not just because he was teasing me about my age. He'd also solved the problem of how I was going to turn the topic to my party without making him suspicious.

"Yeah," I said. "And my party's going to be great, except—" I stopped right there.

"Except what?" my father asked. Just as I had hoped he would. I was beginning to think Arielle was right. Parents were pretty predictable.

"Oh, nothing, it's just—" I shook my head and poked at my peas with my fork. *Ask again*, I willed my father. And he did.

"Just *what*, Felicia?" he said, setting down his fork. He was staring across the table at me, his brow furrowed. I had to hand it to myself. I was better at this scheming business than I had thought I would be. Not that that made it any easier—or made me any less nervous. My palms were all sweaty again, and now my heart was racing, too. Lying to someone's face was even harder than lying over the phone. But either way, I don't think I would have passed a lie detector test.

I shrugged, trying to appear casual. "I just think Mom's kind of stressing about the whole thing," I said.

"Really?" my father asked, watching me intently. "What gives you that impression?"

"I don't know," I said. "I guess just the way she was hurrying around on Sunday, making lists and talking about how much she had to do. And she must have asked me what kind of cake I wanted like five times."

"Huh. That doesn't sound like your mother," Dad said. "She's usually so organized."

"Oh—she's still organized," I blurted. I didn't want him to think that she had gotten all ditzy and flaky like Penny or anything like that. "I think she's just really busy with the bakery. Especially with Blanche on vacation."

"Blanche is on vacation?" my dad asked.

"Yeah," I said. That part was true. And my mom *was* really busy. She just wasn't as stressed out as I was making her sound. "Maybe you should offer to help out," I suggested.

Suddenly, my dad narrowed his eyes at me. *Oops*, I thought. I might have taken it one step too far. I picked up a drumstick and took a big bite out of it so that I wouldn't have to look at him.

"Is there something you're not telling me, Felicia?" my father asked, still staring at me.

"Hmmm?" I mumbled, my mouth full of chicken. I tried to look like I had no idea what he was talking about. "Mm-mmm," I added, shaking my head.

"It just seems to me that if your mother needed help, she'd ask for it," he said.

I swallowed hard. He was right. She would. "Yeah, well—" I started. I was racking my brain to come up with an excuse for her. "Maybe she's been so busy that she just hasn't had a chance yet," I offered.

My dad looked up at the ceiling. "Maybe," he agreed, but he didn't exactly look like he was about to call her up and offer to help out, which was what I needed him to do if I wanted to get the two of them alone.

"So maybe you should call her," I suggested. I shrugged as I said it, as if I didn't really care one way or the other, but I'm not sure my father bought it.

"Felicia," he said. Then he hesitated. Thankfully, Arielle had told me exactly what to do if that happened.

"You know, if you helped out with the decorations and stuff, you could stay for the party. And it would be nice to have you there," I said. He was staring at me again, but this time I didn't look away. Instead I smiled, just like Arielle had said I should. "It would really mean a lot to me," I added, and to my surprise, my father's suspicious look melted away.

"All right," he said with a big sigh. "I'll give your mom a call tonight and see if there's anything I can do." When I heard that, I couldn't help grinning. "But things are different now, Felicia. You know that, right?"

I nodded. "Of course I do," I said. But I also knew that he and Penny weren't talking. And that he had spent forty-five minutes on the phone with my mom the other night. And that my mom missed our South Carolina vacations.

Yeah, things were different, all right. But something told me they weren't all that far from getting back to normal again.

Later that night I was lying on my bed, writing, when I heard my dad laughing. I slammed my journal shut and swung my legs onto the floor. He had to be on the phone. But with whom?

Quietly, I tiptoed to my bedroom door and crept out into the hallway. When I crouched down at the top of the stairs, I could just see his feet on the floor below. He was using the phone just outside the living room, and I could hear everything he was saying.

"I know," he said, still laughing. "I know."

But I don't, I thought. I wished he would say some-thing else so I could figure out who he was talking to.

"That sounds like fun. Maybe we can all go together sometime once things settle down," he added. And then he started laughing again. "Okay. All right. So, then, I'll see you Friday around four?"

Friday? At four?! Oh, my God—he had to be talk-ing to my mom!

"Mm-hmm. No, I'm sure Felicia can get a ride over with Traci or one of the other girls. Okay. Great. And do you need me to bring anything? All right. I'll see you then, Sara. Bye."

I sprang up from my hiding spot and sneaked back to my room, and then I just sort of stood there, grin-ning. I was too excited to lie down and start writing again. I was too excited to do anything.

I could hardly believe it. My dad had been talking to my mom and laughing more than I'd heard him laugh in the last month. He had sounded really happy, and not only that. Apparently, he and my mom had plans to go somewhere together—with me, it sounded like—*once things settled down.* What else could that mean, except that he was breaking up with Penny?

I was ecstatic. Up until I'd heard him say that, I'd kind of just been hoping that maybe they sort of, kind of missed each other and wanted to get back together. But I don't think I had completely believed it—not even when I was arguing with Patrick, which is probably why all of the things he said had upset me so much. Part of me had believed he was right.

But all of a sudden, the idea of my parents getting back together seemed like a real possibility. And with Penny out of the way and Arielle on my side, I realized it just might happen. Soon.

chapter
NINE

From the Desk of Arielle Davis

<u>Possible Dates for Felicia's Party</u>

Brian McFee—

   pros: 8th grader, cute, athletic, popular

   cons: I've never actually talked to him

Mike Repp—

   pros: 8th grader, cute, popular, captain of the basketball team

   cons: his older sister baby-sat for me when I was in first grade—she may have told him embarrassing stuff about me

Trevor Murray—

   pros: cute, popular, great hockey player

   cons: 7th grader, a few months younger than Patrick, so he wouldn't be the oldest guy there

Jack Tolan—

   pros: cute, popular, awesome soccer player

   cons: 6th grader

"Hey, Felicia! Wait up."

Shoot. I pressed my eyes closed. I didn't need to turn around to know it was Patrick calling my name—I recognized his voice. *It's okay*, I told myself. There was nothing he could say that could change what I overheard last night. I just had to remember that.

"Hey, I'm glad I caught up to you," he said. "Where are you headed?"

"English," I said. "Mrs. Scott's room."

"Cool. I have to go that way to get to my class, too. I'll walk with you."

"Okay," I said, even though I really didn't want him to. But what was I going to say? No? You have to walk three feet behind me the whole way? I don't think so.

We walked side by side quietly for a while, which was fine. The hallways were loud enough between classes without us adding our voices to the noise. At least, that's what I thought. But I guess Patrick didn't agree.

"I, um, wanted to . . . well, *apologize* to you, I guess," he said as we rounded the corner to the hall-way where my English class was.

"For what?" I asked, but I didn't look over at him. I just kept walking. I could see Mrs. Scott's classroom door. Twenty more feet and I'd be free.

"For not listening very well yesterday. You know—when you were talking about your parents."

I stopped just short of my English class and stared at him. "Really?" I asked.

"Yeah. I mean, you obviously wanted to talk about it or you wouldn't have brought it up. And I guess I kind of just shot you down, you know? So . . . I'm sorry."

I watched his big brown eyes, unblinking, for a minute. He really seemed to mean it. "That's okay," I said. "Don't worry about it."

"Really?" he asked.

"Yeah," I said, relieved that everything was okay between us. "So, then, you believe me?"

Patrick knit his eyebrows together. "What do you mean?"

"About my parents," I explained. "You said that you shouldn't have shot me down. So that means that you believe me, right? That they might be ready to get back together?"

"Well," Patrick started, "I wouldn't exactly say *that*. I still don't think you should get your hopes up."

Not this again, I thought. "But you just said—"

"I said that I probably could have listened better," Patrick interrupted. "Not that I think you're right about your parents getting back together because I don't. I think you're just setting yourself up to be disappointed, Felicia."

"Well, you're wrong," I shot back. "Because I heard my parents talking on the phone last night, and that's *exactly* what they were talking about—getting back together."

"Felicia, I—"

"I have to get to class," I told him. I didn't need to hear any more of what he had to say. He didn't know my parents, and he didn't know what he was talking about.

"Okay," he said. "Whatever. But look—if things don't, you know . . . *happen* the way you expect them to—"

"I really have to go," I said.

"All right, I just—"

"I'll talk to you later," I told him, and I turned and went into class. But even as I had said it, I knew that the only way I'd be talking to him later was if I didn't see him coming in time to avoid him.

Which is exactly what happened.

Later that day I was standing at Amanda's locker with Traci, Arielle, and Amanda when all of a sudden Patrick was right there.

"Hey, Felicia," he said. Of course, I hadn't told any of my friends that he and I had been fighting, so I'm sure they were all surprised by the cold stare I gave him.

"Hi," I said, without the slightest trace of a smile. I could feel Amanda, Arielle, and Traci—especially Traci—staring at me, but somehow I managed to ignore them.

"Um, I was just wondering if you wanted to go to the arcade again. I want a rematch on that Alien Annihilators game you smoked me at." He gave me a sort of half grin, and I wanted to smile back, but I just couldn't. He was being really sweet and trying really hard, but I knew that once we were alone together again, he'd start lecturing me about how divorced people usually stayed divorced, and that wasn't something I wanted or needed to hear. So I didn't smile. I just stared.

"When?" I asked.

"Well, I have basketball practice until four," he said, "but maybe right after that."

"I can't. We're . . . going shopping," I lied. I glanced around at my friends for support, but Traci and Amanda looked so confused that I was sure they were going to blow it. *Just go along with me*, I begged them with my eyes, but they didn't seem to be getting it. Patrick was sort of squinting at me, like he knew I was lying, and I felt like I was about three inches tall.

Then Arielle threw her arm around my shoulders. "I can hardly wait," she said. "I've been looking forward to it all week." I could have hugged her right there, but I managed to stay cool. "There's a sale at Babe's that we absolutely have to check out, and I need a new pair of shoes. Girl stuff," she said, smiling at Patrick.

"Yeah," he said. "Well, maybe some other time, then."

"Yeah," I said. "Maybe."

He hefted his duffel bag higher onto his shoulder and started down the hall toward the gym. And as soon as he was far enough away, all three of my friends turned to me.

"What was that about?" Traci asked.

And at practically the same time Amanda said, "What's up with you and Patrick?"

"Dish," was all Arielle said, but I knew what she meant. She wanted the scoop. They all did.

"We haven't exactly been getting along well this week," I said.

"That was pretty obvious," Arielle said. "Why not?"

"It's no big deal," I said. "At the arcade yesterday I happened to mention to Patrick that I thought my parents might want to get back together."

"And?" Arielle prodded.

"And he didn't believe me. He thinks I'm getting carried away and setting myself up to be disappointed, and he won't let it go."

"Huh," Arielle said, crossing her arms. "I wonder what his problem is."

"I don't know," I said.

Amanda shrugged.

"Excuse me?" Traci said. All of a sudden she was staring at us all like we'd gone completely insane. "What do you mean, 'what *his* problem is'? You guys are the ones that are making up this whole soap opera just because Penny and Mr. Fiol had one fight."

"It's not just the fight," I said. "There's been a lot of other stuff, too."

"Like what?" Traci said. "The fact that your dad was on the phone with your mom and that your mom said she misses your family vacations? That's not proof. You guys are jumping to conclusions big time."

"No, we're not," I said. "Just last night I heard my dad talking to my mom on the phone again, and he practically said that they were getting back together."

"He did?" Amanda breathed.

"*Practically*," Traci said. "Did you actually hear him say that, Felicia?"

I clenched my jaw. I was getting really tired of having people question everything that I said.

"You didn't, did you?" Traci asked. I just crossed my arms and stared at her. "You see?" she went on. "You're jumping to conclusions."

"Fine," I said. "You can think what you want to think, but I know what I heard, and I know what it means. My parents miss each other, and they're going to get back together."

Traci rolled her eyes. "Well, I think Patrick's right—you're setting yourself up for a big disappointment. I mean, even if your parents do miss each other, that doesn't mean they're going to get back together. My mom misses South Carolina, and so do I, but that doesn't mean we're planning to move back there."

"That's not the same," Arielle said. "You're talking about a place—not a person."

"It is too the same," Traci argued. "Isn't it, Amanda?"

"I don't know," she said quietly, and I thought Traci was going to have a heart attack. She was so used to having Amanda agree with her that she must have been totally caught off guard. "I think Felicia probably knows her parents better than anyone else," she told Traci. Then she turned to me. "But I don't think you should have lied to Patrick," she added. "He was only trying to help."

I was about to agree with her on that one when Arielle interrupted.

"Lie? What lie?" she said. "We really are going shopping, aren't we, Felicia?"

I glanced at Traci just long enough to notice her disapproving stare, but even so, I couldn't help smiling. "Definitely," I said. A pre-birthday shopping spree at the mall was exactly what I needed. And besides, if I could just avoid arguing with Traci and Patrick for one more day, I wouldn't have to worry about it anymore. Because by then, the way my parents felt about each other would be obvious to everyone. And then there would be nothing to argue about.

chapter
TEN

Signboard outside Babe's in the mall

It's Bargain Thursday!
Buy any 3 accessories, get a 4th one free*
*Of equal or lesser value

"How about this?" I asked, holding a bright purple hoop earring with green dots next to my head.

"Beautiful," Arielle said. "But I like these better." She picked up a pair of post earrings that were shaped like monarch butterflies and painted in bright orange and black. "What do you think?"

They were bad enough in her hand, but when she held them up beside her head, I thought I was going to die laughing. "They're . . . the size of . . . tennis balls," I managed between giggles. Arielle checked them out in the mirror, and she burst out laughing, too. But she didn't put them down. Instead she did this crazy walk up and down the aisle, like she was a model in one of those fashion shows that are always on the arts and entertainment channel. Then she started narrating herself.

"Here's Arielle Davis, wearing the hottest new look of the season—butterfly headgear." She walked toward me, pivoted, pivoted again, and then headed back up the aisle, keeping a perfectly straight face the whole time.

"Can you imagine?" she said, setting down the earrings and turning back into herself.

"No," I replied, shaking my head. I tried to visualize her—Arielle Davis, always picture-perfect from head to toe—walking down the hallway of WLMS with those monster butterflies hanging off her head. The image cracked me up all over again.

"Okay, Fiol," Arielle said after a minute. "Pull yourself together. We still have a few more stores to hit, but I can't shop on an empty stomach. Do you want to get some smoothies?"

I wiped the tears away from my eyes and nodded. I was still feeling pretty giggly, and I knew if I tried to speak, I'd just start laughing. So Arielle and I walked over to the food court without talking, ordered our smoothies, and sat down.

"Phew." I sighed. "I haven't laughed like that in a long time."

"Are you sure you're done now?" Arielle asked me.

"Yeah, I'm sure," I said, taking a sip of my raspberry smoothie.

"Good, because I have news. I've decided who I'm going to invite to your party."

"You have?" I said. "Who?"

"Brian McFee. In fact, I already mentioned it to him—just sort of casually on the bus the other day—and he seemed really into it."

"Really?" I asked. Her courage amazed me. I would never dare to approach someone like Brian McFee and ask him out.

"Yeah, he was being really flirty again, so I figured I might as well help him out. I just need to call him tonight to confirm, but I wanted you to be the first to—"

I was in midsip when Arielle suddenly went silent. And white. I swear, her face was the color of flour. "Arielle? What's wrong?"

She didn't answer me. Instead she just stared over my shoulder.

"What is it?" I asked, but she still wasn't responding, so I turned around. And there, just two tables away, was Brian McFee. With a girl. And not just any girl, either. This girl was obviously his *girlfriend*. He had his arm around her, and they were talking and laughing like an old couple.

She wasn't anyone I recognized from school, and suddenly I realized why. She didn't go to our school. She was wearing a Silver Lake Tigers jacket.

So Brian McFee had a girlfriend. But then why would he have been flirting with Arielle? I had turned to Arielle, intending to ask her about it, when all of a sudden the answer hit me. Brian hadn't been flirting with her. Arielle had made it all up.

But that can't be, I told myself. Arielle wouldn't do that. Arielle wouldn't *need* to do that. She could have any guy she wanted. At least, that's the way it seemed. *But maybe*, I told myself, *just maybe . . .*

No. I couldn't believe it. Yet at the same time it was the only explanation that made sense. It would certainly explain why Arielle had been hedging about inviting him all week and why she had refused to ask him in front of me and Traci. And the way she was looking at him now—well, it wasn't exactly the look of someone who'd been played. I mean, if Brian had really been flirting with Arielle and then he'd shown up here with someone else, she'd be mad, wouldn't she? Not humiliated.

But then, suddenly, the look of embarrassment vanished from Arielle's face. "Well," she said, looking and sounding like herself again. "I can't believe him, can you?"

I watched her carefully, worried that she might be close to tears. I know I would have been. "No," I agreed. "I can't."

"Flirting with me when he obviously has a girlfriend," Arielle added, sounding indignant. "What a jerk."

I nodded. "Yeah," I said quietly. I was still expecting her to lose it.

"I should go over there and give him a piece of my mind," she went on. "I would, you know, if it weren't for her."

"Her?" I asked.

"Yeah." Arielle nodded. "His girlfriend. I mean, it's not like she's done anything wrong. She probably doesn't even know what a jerk she's dating."

"No. Probably not," I agreed.

"Well," Arielle said with a sigh. She glanced at me, and I had a feeling she was studying my eyes, trying to figure out just what I was thinking. "He can forget about ever having a shot with me. I guess I'll just have to invite someone else to your party."

"Yeah," I said. "There are a lot of guys that would love to go out with you," I assured her.

"Of course there are," Arielle said. Then she stood up. "I'm just going to duck into the rest room. I'll be right back," she said.

I watched her go, replaying the last few minutes in my head and wondering if I could trust what I thought I had seen, but I knew I had to have been wrong. Because in that brief moment when Arielle had first spotted Brian and didn't seem aware that I was watching her, she had looked just as scared and insecure as I always feel, and that just didn't seem possible.

"I swear, whenever I'm ready on time, my father's always late," Arielle complained. She turned her wrist and checked her watch again, then sighed.

We were sitting on the sidewalk outside the mall, waiting for Mr. Davis to pick us up. So far, we'd only been waiting for about ten minutes, but I had to admit—it *had* felt like a really long time.

In fact, after we'd seen Brian and his girlfriend in the food court, the rest of the afternoon had dragged. Arielle just hadn't been herself. She'd been moody and cranky, which—okay—wasn't exactly *abnormal* for her. But she'd also been quiet and reserved, which definitely was.

"I still can't believe Brian," she started in for about the eighteenth time in the last hour. "I mean, he was totally flirting with me on the bus. You should have heard him. And he was acting like he was completely free. I never would have even considered inviting him to your party otherwise."

"I know," I said. "But you had no way of knowing. It's not your fault."

I inhaled deeply, taking in the scent of fast-food french fries and burgers that always seemed to surround the mall. It was making me really hungry.

"Yeah, but it still makes me mad," Arielle said. I wanted to believe her, but somehow her words didn't ring true. Even as she talked about how mad she was, her slow voice and her flat eyes seemed more sad than angry. "Boys can be such jerks," she added in an unconvincing tone.

"Yeah, they can," I agreed. And I knew that some of them could be. But I had a feeling that Brian hadn't been.

"So," I said, anxious to get off the Brian theme we'd been on all afternoon. "Do you have anyone else in mind for my party?"

Arielle sighed. "I don't know," she said. "I mean, it's such short notice now."

"Still, there are a ton of guys that would jump at the chance to come with you," I said. "All you have to do is pick one."

"Yeah," Arielle said, but she didn't sound very confident. "I don't know. This whole Brian thing has made me so angry that I think I'd be better off just coming alone."

"Really?" I asked. It certainly didn't sound like Arielle. In fact, right now she sounded more like me than she did herself. And somehow I didn't think that coming to my party alone when the rest of us had guys to invite was going to do much for her confidence. If only there was something I could do for her.

chapter
ELEVEN

E-mails sent and received Thursday night:

From: FiFio1
To: FlowerGrl; sockrgrl0; PrincessA
Change of plans! My mom's really stressing about the space in the apartment. Do u think it's 2 late 2 uninvite the guys? I know Patrick will understand. Will the others?

From: FlowerGrl
To: FiFio1; sockrgrl0; PrincessA
I'm kind of embarrassed 2 admit it, but I haven't actually invited Dave yet. I tried, but I couldn't figure out how 2 ask him. U didn't mention it 2 him, did u, Traci?

From: sockrgrl0
To: FiFio1; FlowerGrl; PrincessA
Nope. I didn't say anything 2 Dave. And don't feel bad. I haven't invited Ryan, either. I guess we're a couple of chickens.

From: PrincessA

To: FiFio1; FlowerGrl; sockrgrl0

No problem. I hadn't really decided who to ask yet, anyway.

From: PrincessA

To: FiFio1

U didn't have to do that, u know. I would have been fine. But thanx.

On my way through the lunch line on Friday, I didn't notice anything strange. But when I turned to walk to the table my friends and I usually shared, I nearly dropped my tray.

There had to be something like twenty balloons—red, orange, purple, blue, green—bobbing up and down at the back of the cafeteria. And I knew who had brought them.

"Happy birthday, Felicia!" yelled Arielle as I walked toward her. She was standing on a chair and waving to me, and everyone was staring at her. Or at least they had been, until she called my name. Now they were all staring at me. But for once I was okay with it. Mostly.

I mean, I still felt a little self-conscious, but at least I knew I looked okay. I was wearing my favorite outfit—a V-necked pink shirt with rhinestones, a short black skirt, and chunky black heels. Plus I'd done my hair and makeup the way Arielle had shown me at one of our slumber parties, and I wore a pair of dangly silver earrings with a matching necklace and bracelet that I'd bought at Bagatelle yesterday. And now that Arielle was drawing so much attention to me, I was glad I'd gone to the trouble.

"Hey, there, birthday girl," she called when I got to the table. "This is your chair." Amanda and Traci laughed as Arielle gestured to the chair where most of the balloons were tied.

"Arielle wanted to tie them all there, but Amanda and I convinced her not to," Traci said.

"Yeah—we were afraid you'd float away," Amanda added.

"Thanks," I said, sitting down. It was kind of weird with all those balloons above my head. I kept catching them moving out of the corners of my eyes and getting startled.

"A little jumpy today, huh, Felicia?"

"Who said that?" I called, starting. Then I looked up. It was Ryan Bradley, poking his head through the balloons. "Yeah, just a little," I said.

Traci laughed, and I saw Ryan smile over at her. It was sweet, and it kind of made me wish that Patrick was there, too. But he was sitting at a table with a bunch of his seventh-grade friends, and I wasn't ready to invite him over. Not on my big day. And so far, it had been a big day.

People had been singing "Happy Birthday" to me in all of my classes and even in the hallway. It had caught me off guard at first because I was pretty used to having my birthday come and go without anyone in school really noticing. But this year it was different. Arielle kept showing up outside my classes with balloons—I don't know where she was keeping them all—and people I didn't even know were wishing me a happy birthday. It was kind of weird, but it was really nice, too.

"Okay, guys," I heard Ryan call all of a sudden. "Here we go. One, two, three," he yelled out, and then all at once he started playing "Happy Birthday" on his violin, and his entire table started singing it. And before they had finished, the entire cafeteria had joined in. I could hardly believe it. The whole school was singing to me!

When they were done, everyone cheered, and I could feel my face burning—with embarrassment? Yeah, probably a little. But also with excitement. So far, this was turning out to be the most amazing birthday I'd ever had. But the really incredible thing was that the best part was yet to come.

The best part was going to be seeing my parents together tonight. Especially now that I knew they were on their way to getting back together for good.

I stared in the mirror and carefully went over my eyeliner with a fresh coat. I was actually getting pretty good at putting on makeup. The whole process only took me about twenty minutes in the morning now and only ten or fifteen when I needed to touch it up.

Back when Arielle first taught me how to do it, though, it used to take me a whole hour. And even then it didn't always come out perfectly. But now I had it down pretty well. Still, I was glad it wasn't something I did every day. That would drive me crazy. Once in a while, though, it was fun.

There, I thought when I was done with my lipstick. Now I just needed to fix one clump of hair that kept curling up when it should have been curling down, and I'd be ready.

I picked up my curling iron, but before I could deal with that wild section of my hair, the doorbell rang.

"I'll get it," I yelled, running down the stairs. It was too early to be one of my friends—they weren't coming until later with Ms. McClintic, who was driving us all over to my mom's house.

My dad had arranged it so that my friends and I could ride to the party together once he and my mom had finished getting everything set up. I couldn't help thinking that he wouldn't have gone to all the trouble of finding someone else to drive us if having some time alone with my mom wasn't important to him, too.

Everything is falling into place, I thought as I jogged to the front door. Just before I opened it, I caught a glimpse of three or four balloons through the windows at the top of the door. It could only be one person.

"Arielle, I can't wait to show you—" I started as I swung it open, but when I saw who was standing there, I stopped short.

"Hi, sweetie! Happy birthday," Penny said, smiling and wrinkling her nose at me. "I brought you these." She thrust the balloons forward, but I didn't reach out for them.

"P-Penny?" I stammered.

"Oh, I'm sorry. You were expecting someone else, weren't you?" she said. "I hate when that happens— it's such a disappointment."

I could hardly believe my eyes. What on earth was *Penny* doing here?

"Um, I'm not sure this is a good time," I said.

"Oh, your friends are coming over, aren't they? Well, don't worry," she said, stepping inside and letting the balloons rise to the ceiling. "I'll only be here for a few minutes. Then I'm going to go help your dad with the decorations for your party. You must be so excited."

"Wait a second—did you say you're helping my dad with the decorations?" I asked.

"Yes," she said, clapping. "And they're going to be wonderful, I promise. But that's all I'll say. I don't want to ruin the surprise."

"But . . ." I shook my head. This couldn't be happening. This wasn't right. "You can't help with the decorations," I told her, and Penny laughed. She must have thought I was kidding. "I'm serious," I said, glaring at her. "You can't."

Penny straightened up. "No?"

"No," I said. "My mother's not expecting you."

"She's not?" Penny asked, and I have to say, she looked really hurt, but I didn't care. This wasn't about her, and I wasn't going to let her worm her way into it.

"Ah, Penny," my father said, walking into the foyer. "I thought that was you. I just have a few things to finish up in my office, and then we can head out."

"But Dad," I said. "Penny can't go over to Mom's."

He blinked at me, looked to Penny, and then turned back to me again. "She can't?" he asked. "Why not?"

I exhaled sharply and folded my arms together. "Because no one invited her," I said.

Penny's eyes got really wide and she took a step back, almost as though I'd slapped her across the face with my words.

"Felicia Fiol!" my father barked. "In! My! Office!"

I gave Penny one last sideways glance as I followed my father down the hall and around the corner into his office. "What?" I asked.

For a moment my father stared at me like I was a puzzle he couldn't figure out. Then he sat back on his desk, took a deep breath, and let it out slowly, his features relaxing a little.

"I don't know what's going on here," he said in a low, measured voice, "but I don't like your attitude.

And for your information, *I* invited Penny to your mother's house."

"Why?" I demanded. I knew I sounded more like a pouty five-year-old than someone who had just turned twelve, but I didn't care. He was ruining everything.

"Because your mother thought it would be nice to have Penny helping with the decorations, and I agreed."

"Mom? She wanted Penny to—?" I couldn't even make the words come out. It didn't make sense.

"Yes. Your mother thought that since Penny's an artist, she might have some good ideas—and she did. I think you're really going to like the decorations."

I bit my lip. It was the only way I could keep myself from screaming. The decorations? Did he really think they mattered to me at all? I couldn't have cared less about the stupid decorations. I didn't even care that I was getting lipstick all over my teeth.

"Felicia?" my father said. "Are you all right?"

I nodded. "Yeah, I'm fine."

"You don't look fine," he said. I shrugged. "Is there anything I can do?"

"No," I said. "Just go take care of the decorations. I have to finish getting ready."

"Are you sure?" he asked.

"Yes," I said. "I'm sure."

"All right. But if you need to talk—"

"Don't worry," I told him as I stormed out of the room. "I know where you live."

chapter
TWELVE

Horoscope

Scorpio
Your birthday today: Expect the unexpected.

"Maybe Penny won't be here," Arielle said as my friends and I climbed the stairs to my mother's apartment. Ms. McClintic had just dropped us off after an incredibly quiet ride from my dad's house. No one had really known what to say when I mentioned that my dad had left with Penny, and that was fine with me. Because I didn't feel like talking about it.

"Maybe she was just doing the decorations," Arielle went on, "and now she's gone."

I snorted. It didn't seem likely to me, but Amanda took the idea and ran with it.

"Yeah," she said. "Penny is really good at stuff like that—decorations and everything, I mean. And you said it was your mom's idea, not your dad's. So maybe she really was just helping out. It doesn't have to mean that she and your dad are still together."

"Yeah, right," I muttered. I wanted to believe them. I wanted to think that there was a chance we'd walk into my mom's apartment and everything would be exactly the way I had wanted it to be—my mom and dad standing there together, smiling and wishing me a happy birthday. But somehow I just couldn't imagine it anymore. Instead I was ready to side with Traci, who wasn't saying anything. That seemed like the safest way to go.

When we got to the top of the stairs, the door swung open before I even had a chance to knock.

"Happy birthday!" my mom shouted, all smiles. And to my surprise, my dad was standing right next to her, beaming. My mouth dropped open. They looked perfect together—like they'd stepped right out of a family picture or something.

"Uh, th-thanks," I stammered. Could Amanda and Arielle have been right? I glanced over at them to see that they were gaping, too. They looked as stunned as I was. Even Traci was staring.

"Would you look at our beautiful daughter?" my father said. "She's all grown-up."

Normally I would have groaned, and normally Arielle would have smirked and teased me about that comment later. But I don't think any of us were feeling very normal at that moment.

"You're right, Luis," my mother said. "She's turning into a young lady right before our eyes."

Okay, so I *had* to groan at that one, but I wasn't really upset. I mean, they could have said just about anything to me right then and it would have been fine.

"Penny! The girls are here," my father called.

Anything. But. That.

"Wait until you see what Penny's done in here," my mom said, ushering us in. And there, stirring dipping bowls of guacamole and salsa, was Penny. My heart dropped.

"Oh, hi, sweetie—I mean, Felicia," she corrected herself. Someone must have clued her in to the fact that I didn't like being called cutesy nicknames. I knew she couldn't have figured it out on her own.

"Happy birthday," she added, eyeing me cautiously. "I hope you like the decorations." She waved her arm at the white balloons that covered the floor, the silver spirals that dangled from the ceiling, and the glittery stars and streamers that seemed to be everywhere. Then she waited. And so did everyone else.

It was absolutely silent except for the faint music coming from my mother's stereo. I knew everyone was staring at me, waiting for my reaction. But all I could do was stare. Dumbstruck. With my mouth still hanging open.

"Must be a case of birthday jitters," Arielle said. She linked her arm through mine and addressed my parents and Penny. "It's partly my fault, I have to admit," she went on. "I've been surprising Felicia

121

with balloons all day, and I guess she's a little shell-shocked, huh, Felicia?"

"Uh, yeah," I managed after she elbowed me in the ribs.

"This looks great, Penny," she gushed. "I especially like the glitter inside the balloons. That's such a cool touch."

"Oh," Penny said, obviously surprised by how warmly Arielle was treating her. "Well, thank you, Arielle. You know, I was wondering if—"

"Hey—weren't you going to show me something in your room, Felicia?" Arielle interrupted. And before I could answer, she was pulling me away, heading straight for my bedroom.

Thankfully, no one had a chance to stop us because Traci and Amanda kicked into full gear at that point. As Arielle dragged me off, I heard them going on about Penny's decorations and telling my mother how much they were looking forward to the cake. Then Traci started in on my dad about the shelter and the new dog and Lola's obedience lessons, while Amanda told my mom about the artwork Penny was doing for the skate park.

"Phew," Arielle said, closing my door behind us. "Are you all right?"

I shook my head. "I don't know," I said, and I really didn't. I was still in shock from seeing my parents together and getting my hopes up all over again only to have everything fall apart in front of me. I looked up at Arielle. "Thanks for getting me out of there," I said.

"No problem," she said. "I owed you one."

Just then there was a knock at the door. "Felicia?" It was my mother. "Can I come in?"

"Do you want me to make up an excuse?" Arielle whispered.

I shook my head. "That's okay," I said. "I can handle it."

"You sure?"

I wasn't, but I nodded, anyway.

"Felicia?" my mom called again.

"Yeah. Come on in, Mom," I said, and Arielle opened the door for her.

"Thanks for showing me that . . . *thing*, Felicia," Arielle said as she was leaving. "It was really cool. I'm going to check out the cake, okay?"

"Okay," I said, and I nodded once more to let her know I would be fine. Once Arielle was out, my mother stepped in and shut the door.

"Felicia—what's going on? You seem upset. Are you all right?" She took a seat next to me on my bed and brushed my hair away from my face the way mothers always do.

"Yeah," I lied, "I'm fine."

She studied my face, and I did my best to hide just how disappointed I really was.

"Your father said you got really angry when Penny showed up at his house earlier, but he wasn't sure why. Do you want to tell me about it?"

I blew a puff of air at my forehead. "There's nothing to tell," I said. "I just don't like her."

"Penny?" my mother asked, as if it was a huge shock. Was it that hard to believe that someone could dislike her? As annoying as she was?

I rolled my eyes.

"Oh," my mother said. "I see."

I wondered if she really did.

"Well, I'll admit, she is rather . . . *different,*" my mom said. Boy, that was an understatement. Penny was just plain weird. "But sometimes that can be a good thing," she went on. "Have you talked to your father about it?"

I shrugged. "Not really," I said. But what difference would it make if I did?

"Maybe you should," my mother suggested. "Maybe if you did, he could arrange it so that Penny only came over when you weren't around or something like that. That way you could take it slower and get used to the idea of your dad dating her in your own time."

I stared up at my mom like she was crazy. Get used to Penny? I had no intention of getting used to her. She wasn't going to be around that long. Didn't my mom realize that? Didn't my mom understand that the only person who was right for my dad was *her?*

"You know, Felicia," my mom started, but she was interrupted by the doorbell. "Oh—I'd almost forgotten," she said, sitting up straight. "Well," she said with a sigh, "I guess I'd better get that. But we'll talk more later, okay?"

"Yeah, whatever," I muttered as she rushed out. No sooner had she gone than all my friends rushed in to see how I was holding up.

"What can we do for you?" asked Traci. I glanced up at her, kind of surprised to see just how concerned she was. I'd been giving her grief all week, but still, when I needed her, she was right there. Along with Arielle and Amanda.

"Nothing, really," I said. "I'm fine."

"Are you sure?" Arielle asked. "Because if you want, Amanda can fake a stomachache and get Penny to take her home."

At first Amanda scowled at Arielle, but then she looked at me and sort of shrugged. "I could, you know," she offered.

Now, that wasn't a bad idea, except for the part about Amanda leaving. Penny was the only one I wanted to get rid of. But before I really had a chance to think it over, my mother reached in and knocked on the half-open door.

"Felicia?" she said. "Could you come out? There's someone here I want you to meet."

My friends and I exchanged puzzled looks. Someone

she wanted me to meet? At my birthday party? I slid off my bed and padded out to the living room, surprised to see a strange man standing next to my mother.

"Felicia," she said, "this is Mark."

"Hi," I said, wondering exactly who this Mark guy was.

Then she turned to the man. "And Mark, this is my daughter, Felicia. And these are her friends Arielle, Amanda, and Traci."

"Hello, girls," he said, nodding at my friends. Then, "Hello, Felicia," he said, extending his arm to me. I went ahead and shook his hand. What else was I going to do? "It's nice to finally meet you," he added.

Finally? I thought. What was he talking about?

"Your mother's told me a lot about you."

"She has?" I said, wondering why. Was Mark some new guy she was hiring to help out at the bakery?

"Yes. In fact, when we were having dinner the other night, she happened to mention that you play the flute. My sister plays the flute with the New York Philharmonic."

"Wow, she must be really good," I said, genuinely impressed. Was *that* why my mother wanted me to meet him? Then it hit me. She'd told him about me when they were having dinner the other night. Did that mean . . . ?

My eyes darted to my mother. She must have read my mind because she nodded. "Mark and I have been

126

seeing each other for about a month now, and I thought it was about time that you met him."

For the third time that night my mouth was hanging open and I was speechless. As if having Penny there wasn't bad enough, my mother had brought a date to my birthday party.

chapter
THIRTEEN

From My Personal Book of Lists, by Felicia Fiol

List #33: The Worst Things About Turning 12

1. My dad brought a date to my birthday party.
2. My mom brought a date to my birthday party.
3. My parents are never getting back together.

When everyone was finally gone, I went to my room, closed my door, and collapsed on my bed and cried. Could things have turned out any worse? I, for one, didn't think so. But somehow I'd survived it all—thanks to my friends.

Amanda had kept Penny and my mom busy most of the night talking about the arts budget at WLMS, and Traci had managed to keep my dad talking about the shelter almost nonstop. Of course, I guess that's not all that unusual, considering that the shelter is my dad's favorite topic. But the strange thing was that Mark had gotten really involved in their conversation, too.

I guess he's a real animal lover—unlike Penny. I

heard him say something about working with the Humane Society, but I wasn't sure if he meant that was his job or just some kind of volunteer thing he did, and I wasn't about to go over and ask him. I mean, he seemed like a really nice guy and everything, but I wasn't exactly in the mood to talk to him. Or anyone else. Which is why it was so great to have Arielle there.

She kind of acted as my personal bodyguard all night—jumping in and answering questions for me and pulling me off in a different direction whenever one of my parents got close. I don't know how I would have gotten through this night without her, Amanda, and Traci. I guess that was something to be thankful for.

Unfortunately, all I could think about were the bad things that had happened. Penny showing up at my dad's house. Penny being at the party. My mom introducing me to her . . . *boyfriend*, or whatever Mark was. And of course, the worst one of all: realizing how wrong I'd been about my parents.

I pulled another Kleenex out of the box by my bed and blew my nose. Then I crumpled up the tissue and tossed it on the ground with the thousands of others that were already there.

I just didn't get it. How could I have been so off base? How could I have read into everything so much? My parents had been apart for two years now. I thought I was over that stuff. Had I actually believed they were going to get back together? *Yeah*, I thought. *I did*. But not anymore. Now I knew the truth. That it was never going to happen.

Another wave of sadness swept through my body. I pressed my eyes shut and got ready for the tears to flow again, but they didn't come. I guess I didn't have any more left. I grabbed a tissue and wiped at my nose anyway, though.

"Felicia?"

I jumped at the sound of my father's voice. "Dad?" I said, sounding all scratchy and stuffed up. My mother had gone down to the bakery to prep for tomorrow, and I had thought I was alone in the apartment. But I guess not.

"Yeah," he answered. He pushed open my bedroom door just far enough to stick his head through. "Can I come in?"

"Sure," I said, trying to sound like I hadn't been sobbing for the last half hour. Quickly, I gathered up all of the tissues and stuffed them into my trash. Then I grabbed one more and dried my eyes and nose as much as I could.

"I thought you had left," I said to my dad when he sat down next to me on the bed.

He nodded. "I did—I took Penny home. But I wanted to come back and make sure you were all right."

"Oh. Well, I'm fine," I lied, keeping my eyes trained on the floor. If he saw just how puffy they were, he'd never believe me.

"You don't look fine," he said. "And I think I know why."

That got my attention. I looked up at him and narrowed my eyes. "Why?" I asked.

"Because of Penny," he said. Well, he was half right. "And Mark," he added. I tilted my head, still staring at him. "And the fact that your mom and I aren't together anymore."

I felt a huge lump forming in my throat and thought that maybe my supply of tears had built up again. I looked away from my father and blinked a few times to keep them from rolling out.

"It must be hard for you to see us both with new people all of a sudden, huh?" he asked.

"I guess," I managed to say. I closed my eyes, but there was no stopping the tears now.

"Hey," my dad whispered, putting his arm around me and holding me close. "It's okay, Fifi. It's okay."

Fifi. A little laugh escaped in the middle of my crying when I heard him use that name. It's what he'd always called me when I was a little girl. In fact, he had called me that right up until last year, when I had started complaining that it sounded like a name for a dog. Now he only used it when he was joking with me. *Or,* I thought, *when he's treating me like I'm still his little girl.*

He held me while I cried, rubbing my back and whispering, "It's okay, Fifi," and "I love you," over and over again. And as upset as I was, it felt good to cry—to just let it all out.

"It's just hard," I rasped when I finally had the crying under control.

"I know it is," my dad said. "Especially when your parents bring dates to what's supposed to be their reunion party."

I hung my head, too embarrassed to even look at him. I couldn't believe that I'd actually been thinking of my birthday party that way. "You figured that out?"

"Yeah, but not soon enough. If I'd known that's what you were thinking, I never would have invited Penny. And your mother wouldn't have picked tonight to introduce you to Mark, either. That was pretty bad timing on our part, huh?"

I nodded. It sure was.

"But what I don't understand," my father said, "is what made you think your mom and I were getting back together. We've been divorced for two years."

"I know," I said. "But you had that fight with Penny."

"On Monday?" he asked.

"Yeah."

"That wasn't a *fight*," he said.

"It sure sounded like one," I told him. "When Penny left, I thought you two had broken up."

"Ahhh," my father said. "Yeah. I guess I can see how it might have looked that way. But Penny and I worked everything out before Officer Smith showed up with that dog. Penny only left because I had work to do."

"Yeah, well. I get that now," I said. "But—what about that conversation you had with Mom? The one where you said, 'Maybe we can all go together sometime once things settle down'?"

My father furrowed his brow. "Felicia Fiol. Were you eavesdropping?"

"*No-ooo,*" I said, squirming a little. "You were just talking really loud." He shot me a disapproving look, and I knew he didn't believe me. But I also knew he wasn't about to discipline me for it now.

"Anyway," I said. "What did you mean?"

My father chuckled. "Your mother had gone bowling with Mark, and I thought that maybe it would be fun if Penny and I went with them sometime."

"But you said 'once things settle down'—what did you mean by that?"

"Just that your mom's been really busy at the bakery with Blanche gone and your birthday party to plan. I figured things would settle down for her in another week or so, and then maybe we could make plans for the four of us to get together."

"Oh," I said. Wow—I'd really taken that the wrong way. I guess that was the problem with eavesdropping.

"You know, Felicia, your mom and I had a lot of good times together. But the best part of our fifteen years together was having you."

I kind of felt like I should say thank-you or something, but I didn't have it in me.

"We've always loved you, we've always been proud of you, and we've always worked together to be the best parents we can be to you. And that's never going to change. So in a way, your mom and I always will be together—as your parents."

"I know," I said.

"But," my father went on, "that doesn't make it any easier to see us both moving on with new people, does it?"

I wiped a tear away from my eye. "No," I said quietly.

"Well, I apologize for not being more sensitive about that," he said. "I think maybe I've been pushing a little hard for you to get to know Penny, and maybe I need to back off on that. Would that help?"

"Maybe," I said.

"And Penny had an interesting suggestion, too," he added. *Darn. Just when I was starting to feel a little better,* I thought. "She and I had planned to come by tomorrow and take you out to lunch—"

"Dad, I'm not sure—"

"Let me finish," he said, holding up his hand. "But instead Penny thought it might be nice if we took a weekend trip to Chicago—just you and me."

I squinted at him. I couldn't have heard that right. "Chicago?" I said. "You and me?"

My dad nodded. "Yeah," he said. "It just so happens that Penny had a couple of tickets to a performance of *Annie Get Your Gun* that's going on at one of the theaters in town. The owner at the gallery where she just had a show gave them to her, and she suggested that I take you."

"Penny came up with that?" I asked.

"Yeah—she even mentioned that there was a museum of modern art there that you might be interested in and a Hard Rock Cafe where we could have lunch."

"The Hard Rock Cafe?" I asked. I'd always wanted to go there. It sounded so cool, and it seemed like I was the only person around who'd never been to one.

"Uh-huh." My dad grinned. "Penny thought you'd like that." I started to scowl, and he quickly added, "Not that that's important—I mean, what Penny thought. I'm not trying to get you to like her. I just thought it was a good suggestion."

He was backpedaling so fast that I almost felt sorry for him. At least I knew he'd meant what he said about not pushing Penny on me anymore. And even though I hated to admit it, Penny *had* come up with a really good idea.

"So what do you say?" my father asked. "You, me, Chicago—does that sound like a good birthday weekend?"

Well, what was I going to say? *No?* I don't think so.

About a half hour later I was writing in my diary when the phone rang. I didn't bother to answer it because I figured I'd just seen all of my friends an hour ago, and they probably wouldn't be checking in on me that quickly.

But to my surprise, my mom came in a second later and told me it was for me.

"Hello?" I said, picking up my phone.

"Hey, Felicia. It's Patrick."

"Patrick?"

"Yeah. I, uh, hope you don't mind that I called."

"No," I said quickly. "Not at all. I'm just . . . surprised." After the way I'd been avoiding him the last couple of days, I kind of figured he wouldn't want anything to do with me.

"Oh, well . . . I just wanted to say happy birthday. I didn't really get a chance to in school today."

I closed my eyes and sighed. I'd seen him walking up to me by my locker after lunch, but I'd just pretended not to and walked the other way. "Thanks," I said, feeling like a total jerk. How could I have been so rude to him?

"And I also wanted to apologize."

I was stunned. "You? Apologize? What for?"

"I don't know," he said. "For getting you so upset, I guess. Two days in a row."

"Oh, Patrick—I'm the one who should be apologizing." The next part was going to be hard to say, but I knew I had to do it. "You were right."

He hesitated. "I was—what do you mean?"

"About my parents," I said. "They're not getting

back together—not even close. They both had *dates* for my birthday party."

"Whoa," he said. "That bites."

I giggled. That was one thing I really liked about Patrick. He said what was on his mind. "Yeah, it did," I admitted. "But it wouldn't have been so bad if I hadn't convinced myself that they were going to get back together. I should have listened to you."

"Nah," he said. "You were right not to. I'm usually wrong."

"No, you're not," I said, giggling again.

"That's what my sister says," he said, and we both laughed.

"So," I said, after a minute. "Can you forgive me for being such a jerk to you this week?"

"I don't know," he said. "I guess that depends."

My heart skipped a beat. "On what?" I asked.

"On whether or not you plan to give me another chance to beat you at Alien Annihilators. The last time we played, you killed me."

I heaved a sigh of relief. For a second there I thought he was really upset with me. "Yeah, I'll give you another chance," I told him. "But I'm not going to let you win."

"I wouldn't want you to," Patrick said, and I smiled. *Having him for a boyfriend wouldn't be such a bad thing after all*, I thought. But I still wasn't sure I was ready to say it out loud.

chapter
FOURTEEN

From My Personal Book of Lists, *by Felicia Fiol*

<u>List #34:</u> The Best Things About Turning 12, Revisited

1. Traci gave me a collage that she put together with all kinds of pictures from my summers on the South Carolina coast with her. It was so cool! I hung it up on my wall right above my desk so I can look at it every time I sit down to study.
2. Amanda drew this awesome picture of me playing with some of the dogs at the shelter. She's really an amazing artist. Dad said we could get it framed and put it up in the living room.
3. Arielle gave me the new Shauna Ferris CD and a gift certificate to the mall so we can go shopping again soon.
4. I had an awesome day with my dad yesterday. We went up to the top of the Sears Tower and had burgers, shakes, and fries at the Hard Rock Cafe. He even got me a T-shirt there. Oh, and the show Penny gave us tickets for was really good. I guess I should thank her.
5. My parents may not be getting back together, but at least they're always going to be there for me—both of

them. And i guess i'm pretty lucky that they get along so well, too. Not to mention that they both have cool jobs where i can hang out with my friends. All in all, i guess life is pretty good.

On Friday when I had walked into the cafeteria, I hadn't noticed the balloons at all. But today they caught my eye immediately.

"Um, Arielle?" I said as I walked up to our table. "My birthday was Friday, remember? What are you doing?"

"Apologizing," Arielle said.

Amanda stepped forward and handed me a flower. "Me too," she said. I squinted at Traci, who was sitting down eating her lunch, and she just shook her head.

"Apologizing for what?" I asked, looking back and forth between the two of them.

"Well, I was thinking about it all weekend," Arielle said.

"And so was I," Amanda put in.

"And I feel horrible," Arielle went on.

"Yeah. Me too," Amanda agreed.

I scrunched up my face. "*What* are you two talking about?" I asked.

"Your parents," Arielle said. "I was the one who got you thinking that they were going to get back together, and I was totally wrong. I blew everything way out of proportion—your dad's fight with Penny, that comment your mom made about missing vacations. And after your party, well, I realized that I got all worked up about nothing and ended up really hurting you."

She'd gone on for so long that *I* felt out of breath. "Arielle," I started, but Amanda jumped in again.

"Yeah, and I shouldn't have been so encouraging," she said. "I guess I just wanted it to be true, too. Not just your dad and Penny breaking up, but your parents getting back together. It just seemed so . . . *possible*."

"I know," I said. "I was pretty convinced, too."

"Which is why I'm apologizing," Arielle said. "Because I'm the one who convinced you. And to make it up to you, I'm going to throw you another birthday party—a huge one—and I'm inviting the whole school. We can have it at my house, and I'm going to get a band and a few—"

"Arielle," I said. "You don't have to do that."

"Yes, I do," she said. "I totally ruined your birthday for you, and I want to fix it. My mom can call that guy who does the ice sculptures and we can—well, what do you like better? Castles or skaters? He can do both."

"*Arielle*," I said again, and now I was laughing. "Really—I don't need another party. I had a great day with my dad in Chicago on Saturday."

"Yeah, but—"

"But nothing," I said. "You weren't trying to hurt me. You were trying to help me. And so were you," I added, turning to Amanda. "And besides—both of you more than made up for it by helping me get through that night. I couldn't have done it without you."

Amanda blushed and stared down at her feet. And I could be wrong, but I think Arielle was blushing a little bit, too.

"And *you*," I said, turning to Traci.

She sat bolt upright and stared at me. "What did I do?"

"Oh, nothing," I said, "except help me through one of the worst nights of my life without once saying, 'I told you so.'"

Traci shrugged one shoulder. "That's what friends do," she said. I smiled. Then I looked at Amanda and Arielle, and they both nodded. Traci was right. That was the kind of stuff friends did for each other.

And as I stood there in the cafeteria, multicolored balloons bobbing above my head, I realized that with my three best friends around to help me out, there wasn't anything I couldn't get through.